You Can't Get There From Here

PARLIAMENT SQUARE SERIES
BOOK ONE

You Can't Get There From Here

a sarah jennings novel

Elaine C. Baumbach

SPANGLER PRESS

YOU CAN'T GET THERE FROM HERE
Parliament Square Series
Book One
A Sara Jennings Novel

Copyright 2018
By Elaine C. Baumbach

Email: Elaine@ElaineBaumbach.com
Facebook: Elaine Montchal Baumbach

Spangler Press

ISBN 978-0-578-42859-8

LCCN 2018914450

Printed in the United States of America.

Dedication

To my Grandchildren—Cashe, Peyton and Shawn
Being a Grandparent is so much more fun than being a parent. It's too bad we can't have our grandchildren first.
My Grandmother Motto: "Always remember—What Happens at Grammy's Never Happened!!!"

Table of Contents

Molly's Place Rescue
About the Author

Acknowledgments

When seven candles appeared on my birthday cake, each representing a decade of my life, I questioned how I could possibly be that old. I didn't feel that old (most days). I didn't act that old (no rocking chair or cane yet). I didn't look that old (so I am told). The cruel reality was that, in doing the math, I was that old.

My goal to write a novel could wait no longer. The desire lived within me for what seemed like a lifetime but it was overshadowed by life's demands decade after decade. It was indeed time to put my thoughts on paper and turn that goal into a reality. This book is the product of that aspiration.

Over the months I created the manuscript chapter by chapter. I needed feedback and editing from actual readers to assist me in the process so I enlisted friends to travel with me on my literary journey. They provided me with the encouragement and the kind and supportive words I needed to hear.

Below is a list of those friends who donated their time and energy to edit each chapter as it was written. Each review was greatly appreciated and inspired me to continue. Their enthusiasm for a *Parliament Square* series to follow this book was overwhelming.

Barbara D'Agostino

James Mitchell

Betsy Wray DeStefano

Melanie Davis

Deb Bolls

Pam Wirt

Diane Calhoon

Ray Protzman

Jan Stahlman

Sue Clausen

Jean Jama

Susan Straub

With the assistance of my editor, Jason Liller of Liller Creative, LLC, my ambition to have this book published was made possible. Chapter by chapter he polished my original manuscript creating the best possible product prior to publication. His numerous years of experience in the literary field enabled our author/editor relationship to grow and flourish through the process.

Be advised that the aging process takes no prisoners. Procedures are available to improve physical appearance by camouflaging the side effects of increasing chronological age but they do not alter actual age. Those lucky enough to live into their seventies, eighties, nineties and beyond must learn to accept the fact that happiness cannot be given by others, it comes from within and is truly a personal choice.

Preface

Who hasn't chuckled at an episode of the bumbling *Golden Girls*? The 2018 sitcom *The Cool Kids* shows the humorous side of life in a senior living community. Two recent movies, *Book Club* and *Our Souls at Night*, bring the geriatric generation to the forefront. The senior adult population is constantly growing. Medical advances, fitness programs and social venues targeting those in their golden years have allowed senior citizens to live longer and remain active and involved. This is not your father's retirement life.

The really lucky ones will be afforded health, wealth and the ability to reside at their residence of choice with little or no outside assistance until their expiration date is met.

Some voluntarily or through family intervention will be moved to a senior-living facility to live out their remaining years in a community of older adults. The unfortunate will succumb to illness, poverty, loneliness or some combination of the three.

There is no way to cheat death. One day it will come knocking for each one of us. The best one can hope for is to deter the Grim Reaper for as long as possible while living a life that is purposeful, comfortable and relatively free of mental and physical disabilities.

As the aging process becomes a reality, memories and words of older family members who are no longer with us come to mind. When we were the younger members of the family, we often listened but didn't fully connect to what they were saying or doing. Now a blinding flash of the obvious consumes us as we realize that we have become them.

It can be a real wake-up call to fully comprehend that in the normal progression of life, your number is the next one to be called. The reflection looking back at you in the mirror is that of a parent or a grandparent. It certainly cannot be you!

Younger readers will hopefully empathize with seasoned adults while older readers will directly relate. Life is all a matter of prospective based on our current age which provides our looking glass into what the future holds.

The majority of the population hopes to get to Heaven, but very few are willing to give up their mortal life to get there. A thought to ponder at any age, in the words of Mark Twain, is "The fear of death follows from the fear of life. A man who lives fully is prepared to die at any time." Something to think about!

Life presents us with many crossroads where difficult choices must be made. Sometimes our decisions are good, sometimes our decisions are inconsequential, and sometimes our decisions are bad. The *what if* moments in our lives are much like those in the life of Sara, the protagonist of this book. In most cases our choices cannot be changed because do-overs are rarely an option.

As you read this book, you will discover *what if* moments sandwiched between the current-day happenings at the Parliament Square senior-living community. At times it may be difficult to remember which events are real and which are not. Think about some of the *what if* moments in your life. Which decisions would you change given the opportunity? If you could turn back the hands of time, would you?

Note from the Author

Young adult is the hot genre in fiction right now. This book is in the somewhat more cool-to-the-touch *seasoned, mature adult* genre. In other words, it's written for people who forget why they walk into a room, look for their cell phone while they're talking on it, and are members in good standing of The Lost Glasses Support Group. If any of this describes you, today is your lucky day. If you find yourself scratching your head trying to remember what happened three chapters ago, never fear: Just turn to the *Addendum* at the end of the book. It includes a cast of characters and a chapter-by-chapter summary to refresh your memory and get you back up to speed quickly.

Sara is on the next page, anxious to meet you. I hope you enjoy your stay at Parliament Square.

Chapter One: Transition

the beginning

The years melted together into a lifetime of events, leaving no experience unrelated to the many others around it. Where had all the expectations gone? How did all the yesterdays lead to today? And in the journey of life, what was yet to come? Sara's mind raced as she sat quietly in the large lobby waiting for Michael, her nephew, to return. Her hands folded on her lap, her precious cat Penelope resting in the cage by her feet, she feared what was happening but accepted that it was what must be.

All her tomorrows were woven into the fabric of today. How she wished this could all be but a bad dream and she would awaken to the comfort and security of her cozy cottage by the sea. But there were no seagulls calling to her for scraps of bread nor could she hear the soothing, rhythmic lapping of the ocean's waves on the sandy beach. Yet another memory of what was no more. She tried hard to be brave and not allow anyone to see the pain she felt deep inside, but the feeling of hopelessness gnawed at her heart like mice devouring a block of cheese. How she ached for yesterday. How she hated today. How she feared tomorrow.

Michael's patience with Aunt Sara could best be described as infinite. When he first mentioned to her that he was shopping for safe, comfortable and affordable senior living facilities in Massachusetts within a fifty mile radius of his residence, she was adamant about not being interested.

As the months passed, her eyesight became a bit compromised and her pace began to decelerate; he once again presented her with viable options. She had to admit that although her first choice would be to leave her cottage on a gurney after departing this world peacefully in her sleep, the time had come to listen to reason. She no longer had the physical strength and stamina needed to maintain the property. Michael helped her with many tasks over the past couple of years but he had a job, his own home and a wife. She could no longer take advantage of his kindness or afford to pay a service. As hard as it was for her to accept, it was time.

There were many levels of senior-living communities. Sara certainly did not need memory care nor did she require an assisted-living level of care. She needed an environment which supported independent living with minimal monitoring, senior neighbors and sustainable age-appropriate activities and events. After an extremely thorough search and much research, Michael chose Parliament Square. This facility would allow his aunt to live comfortably among her peers and provide him with peace of mind knowing that she was no longer living an isolated and dangerous existence at her beloved cottage by the sea.

After what seemed like hours as her mind wandered back in time, but may have only been minutes, Michael returned from the office after picking up the key to Aunt Sara's apartment. He discussed the next step in the day's journey. The paperwork had been completed and the newly painted and carpeted room where Sara and Penelope would reside awaited her arrival. The time had come to take that next step, the step she had been reluctant to take for quite some time but the step that had become evident over the past several months to be necessary.

Michael moved all her worldly belongings into the Parliament Square Retirement Village. She departed her home of the past forty-plus years and the memories that resided in every corner of that dwelling to begin a new chapter in her life, a chapter that not only petrified her but a chapter that she never wanted to write. A chapter scripted for old people who were infirm and unable to take care of their own daily affairs, but not a chapter for her. A chapter that David said would never be written during his lifetime. But David was gone and Sara felt deserted, forlorn, and most of all scared.

Slowly, Sara rose from the lovely flowered sofa, which had an oddly pleasant disinfectant aroma. With every ounce of courage she could muster, she followed Michael. Penelope meowed as he carried the cage toward the elevator. How would Penelope adapt to her new surroundings? She would no longer have the lovely ocean view from the window seat which was her favorite place during their eight years together. She would no longer playfully bat at the window as the seagulls swirled outside looking for stale bread crumbs in the yard. Ahead lurked a difficult and life-changing adjustment for both of them.

The elevator opened revealing two female residents who were complaining that there hadn't been enough syrup for the breakfast pancakes and that they made the coffee too strong. When they saw Sara and Michael they said "Hello!" and peeked into Penelope's carrier to offer several "kitty, kitty" greetings. They admired the beautiful green color of the cat's eyes watching them through the opening. "Her name is Penelope," Sara said one decibel above a whisper. "No offense, but she doesn't like strangers and neither do I. This is a very difficult day for us." Sara maintained her sober expression; today was indeed a sobering experience.

If only she had been fortunate enough to gasp her last breath in her own home and never have to make this difficult transition. But she had outlived her ability to reside independently there because of her age-related macular degeneration and arthritic joints. It could be a lot worse; after all, her thought processes and mental faculties remained intact.

The cottage by the sea required a younger person's energy, eyesight and physical abilities. Michael felt that it was in her best interest to move to a facility that could accommodate her needs and provide for her safety. She cursed under her breath at the situation but remained audibly silent during the ride to the building's third floor.

The door opened and Michael helped Sara and Penelope from the elevator. The two women bid Sara a good day and again welcomed her to the village. Sara only nodded as she reluctantly stepped into the hall. She found it difficult to render a smile on this day. She slowly followed Michael and Penelope to a door festooned with a colorful flowered wreath and marked with the room number: 316. Again the smell of disinfectant was evident but not overwhelming.

As Michael unlocked the door, Sara braced herself for the worst. She pictured a hospital-like room with medicinal and institutional qualities. She was pleasantly surprised to instead see a cheerful sunlit suite filled with her precious possessions. Michael arranged for the transition to take place while he accompanied Aunt Sara on a trip to visit out-of-state relatives the previous week. He hoped it would lessen the negative impact of the event and allow Sara to more quickly acclimate to her new surroundings.

Michael made every effort to cushion and protect Aunt Sara as if she were a young child going away from home for the very first time. Although he had been diligent in his efforts to make this process as painless as possible, he felt that he had failed his aunt as he saw the sadness on her face as she entered her new home.

Her unhappiness was out of character. Sara had been a pillar of strength for Michael during his youth. She had always been there to encourage him when he struggled with school or girls or sports. She taught him how to be strong when he felt weak and vulnerable. She had even been a role model for him as she struggled with David's unexpected passing, a time when her external strength and resilience hid her internal devastation. Now the tables had turned and it was Michael's turn to be strong for Aunt Sara. At this moment, he questioned his ability to make a difference.

Once inside the apartment, Michael placed the carrier on the floor and opened the door to allow Penelope to escape from her cramped travel quarters. She emerged slowly and cautiously, stretching out her body, relieved to be free of the carrier's confinement. Within minutes Penelope positioned herself on the large window sill overlooking the gardens below. Although there were no sea gulls circling outside, other birds chirped and flew past the window. How simple life would be if people could adapt to change as easily as animals.

One of Michael's requirements for his aunt's new home was the ability to have pets. Separating Sara and her beloved Penelope would have been inhumane. They were the best of friends and Michael often overheard Sara's conversations with Penelope on her cottage porch. He would chuckle at the banter back and forth between them knowing that his aunt used that two-way conversation to fill the void in her life for companionship with friends and family. Her independent ways had once been her forte. Now, stripped of that independence, she felt fragile and helpless.

Michael conducted a tour of the residence, accentuating the positive and sidestepping the negative. The suite included a complete kitchen so she could make her own breakfast and lunch and only join the other residents in the dining room for her evening meal. The bedroom was spacious with large windows, access to the veranda and a roomy walk-in closet. The nicely sized dining/living room accommodated much of Sara's furniture including her prized piano. The bathroom housed a walk-in shower with safety features including a call button for emergencies.

Sara followed Michael emotionlessly through the rooms. She was overwhelmed with all the changes and unhappy with the transition. She just wanted to sit with Penelope on her lap, fold her arms and have a good cry. She wanted to express the pain and suffering that this change caused her but she was much too polite to show how she felt in front of Michael. He worked so hard to make this as painless as possible and she didn't want to appear ungrateful.

If Michael had not been there to take over the sale of the house, the packing, the search for her new residence, the mountains of paperwork, she would have been adrift and helpless. Without any children of her own, Sara was indeed lucky to have Michael and grateful for all his assistance.

Sara had often fantasized about what her children would have been like. If she had a daughter would she be like Sara or would she be more flamboyant and adventuresome? Would she have scooped Sara up in her loving arms and demanded that she come live with her and her family at this time of crisis? Would she have been surrounded by grandchildren begging for her attention and affections while offering theirs? These questions had no answers.

Michael promised to go to the dining room with Sara for dinner. She wanted to simply stay in her room with Penelope purring on her lap but Michael reminded her that she had to eat to keep up her strength. It would be fun, he told her. She would get to meet new people, make new friends and begin writing a new chapter in her book of life. She wanted to scream at the top of her lungs "This is NOT what I want. I would rather be DEAD. I would rather be reunited with my dear, sweet David. I don't want to go on. I don't want another chapter in my life." But she remained silent and waited patiently until Michael escorted her to the dining area.

Sara remembered how, when she was young, she used to think it silly to eat dinner so early, when restaurants advertised their early-bird specials and filled their seats with senior citizens. Now she was one of those senior citizens and dinner started promptly at 5:00 PM. Eating so early made the evening seem endless.

When she was living alone, she would eat whenever she was hungry. It might be at 5:00 but more frequently it was around 6:00 when the local nightly news was on. Although many of today's news stories can give one indigestion, she still thought it was good to keep up with current events. Sometimes she would wait until 7:00 so she could guess along with the contestants on the evening game shows. Those programs were easier on the digestion.

There were no televisions in the main dining room. There were about twenty tables, each with place settings for eight people. They had linen tablecloths and real china dishes. Nice touch, she thought. Each resident was assigned to a table and until one of those diners left the village, for one reason or another, those seven would be the residents Sara shared her evening meal with every day. The room was tastefully decorated and the waitstaff were all young, probably students at the local community college.

Sara remembered passing the college on their drive to the village. She thought how wonderful it would be if she could turn back the clock and be one of them... ready to start out on a lifetime of adventures instead of waiting for death to come knocking on her door. She literally shook her head to erase the thought. Youth was so underrated until it left you standing in an old person's body wondering *How did this happen?* She finally decided what she wanted to be when she got older—wait for it—she wanted to be younger!! If only it were that simple.

As they walked to her assigned table, she caught their reflection in a wall covered entirely with mirrors. Michael was a handsome man. He had a slender build for his tall frame. Sara could easily fit under his arm when they stood side by side. David had always teased her about her petite stature, saying she was height-challenged. It got even worse with age; diminished height was yet another negative side effect of the aging process. She wondered if the other diners thought he was her son. That would be fine with her because she often thought of Michael as the son she never had. She was glad to be on his arm.

Sara and Michael were the first two seated at the table. It was close to the doors leading outside, so that was nice. The nearby window allowed an outside view so she could see the sun before it set on the horizon.

Soon others began to join them. The first was a woman whose skin appeared to be weathered from a lifetime of sun exposure prior to the availability or promotion of sunscreen. Sara remembered when people used to spend all day in the sun without coating themselves from head to toe with sunscreen. Sometimes they would spread baby oil on their skin to darken their tans, the sun frying them like chicken in a pan. My, how things have changed, she thought. The woman introduced herself as Mary and welcomed Sara to the village with a simple "Hello" and a quick al-dente-noodle handshake.

Next was Pam who made her way to the table with the assistance of a walker adorned with dozens of kitty decals and an annoying bell that sounded like the ice cream truck of days gone by. Pam spoke loudly as if she had trouble hearing and thought everyone around her did too. Pam called Sara *Tara* and, after correcting her several times, Sara just let it go. Pam, using her outside voice, boomed "GLAD TO MEET YOU TARA. WE LOVE HAVING A NEW PERSON ASSIGNED TO OUR TABLE. THE FUNERAL FOR OUR OLD TABLEMATE WAS JUST LAST WEEK." Oh, that was more than Sara needed to know and something the entire dining room probably heard.

This is going to take some getting used to, Sara thought. Was she really the same age as these people? Although she realized her eyesight was somewhat impaired and the aging process

9

left her with more aches and pains with each passing year, she still didn't feel old. Maybe it was all a matter of perspective.

Jan was the next to be seated. She wore a Mickey Mouse sweatshirt and her hair looked like she had just seen a ghost, put her fingers in an electric socket or recently been tasered. Sara wasn't sure how she could keep her hair in that position or why she would want to, but no one else at the table seemed to notice. Sara thought this must be normal for Jan and introduced herself.

Jan was a hugger and immediately gave Sara a hug that many bears would be jealous of getting. Sara regained normal breathing shortly afterward. Then Jan gave Michael a hug too. He accepted, but fought to keep it within limits. Sara hoped this was a "glad to meet you" hug and not a nightly event.

Jan turned to Pam and said "You need to learn to speak more quietly and the lady's name is Sara not Tara for heaven's sake." Then Jan winked at Sara and whispered, "Cuckoo for Cocoa Puffs" and made a circular motion with her finger above her right ear.

Jim introduced himself and took the chair next to Michael, probably hoping to engage him in some sport-related conversations during dinner. Jim appeared to be in good health and offered a firm handshake. Sara was so glad that he was not another hugger; she was still catching her breath from Jan's. Jim's voice was deep and had what Sara thought sounded like a slight Southern lilt. "Sara, it is truly a pleasure to meet you, and allow me to speak for my tablemates when I say welcome, welcome, and welcome. To lighten the mood, I have a bit of humor to share with my dining companions this evening. According to most studies, people's number-one fear is public speaking. Number two is death. Death is number two. Does that sound right? This means the average person, if attending a funeral, would rather be in the casket than doing the eulogy." Laughter rang out.

Jim wore khaki cargo pants with a short-sleeve animal-print shirt. He was tanned and appeared to be athletic for his senior status. He was one of the few men in residence with a full head of hair. At least it appeared to be his own hair, but who can tell anymore? He was outgoing and could keep the conversation going no matter who he was with.

It was clear from the gathering crowd that the women outnumbered the men by quite a margin at the village. The table filled quickly; only three seats remained. Sara made mental notes about each person. They would be her daily dining companions and she wanted to remember everything she could about each one. They say older people cannot remember well but Sara disagreed. She felt her mental faculties were still as functional as ever and wanted to prove that to everyone at the table. She was only here because her nephew feared for her safety when she was alone and, although she respected his concerns, she did not totally agree with them.

Diner number six was a well-dressed woman with perfectly coiffed hair and recently manicured nails. Basically she was the opposite of Jan. Sara found it interesting that these two uniquely different individuals were seated at the same table. Sara wondered how the "powers that be" made the executive decisions about table seating. Did they put all the residents' names in a hat and randomly decide the diner's destiny based on a simple name-pull? Or was it discussed around a boardroom table with all the administrative types casting ballots to decide each diner's fate? Maybe it was determined by the location of the resident's rooms or their age or some other defining human attribute. Sara would never know but it was a question she found interesting to ponder.

The fashion-plate woman was introduced as Deborah. Not Deb, not Debbie, no: *Deborah*. From all external appearances, Deborah presented herself as a resident of affluence who would look perfect whether she was at dinner or sitting on the dock of the bay. Sara guessed that she went to bed looking like this and awoke each morning in the same pristine condition. Deborah was quiet and took her seat with little or no communication with the other diners. "A pleasure to meet you," was her brief message to Sara.

It was getting close to the official 5:00 dinner time and two seats at the table were still vacant. Sara noticed a flurry of activity near the entrance. A gregarious woman almost jogged to the table with her curly locks still damp from the shower. She was dressed in wool even though the temperature was enough to make someone dressed in a cotton short-sleeved blouse perspire. Elizabeth was her name and the other residents called her Betsy.

Betsy's effervescence could give a shaken soda bottle a run for its money. She said passing hellos to residents at other tables as she bounced through the room, moving like Tigger in a *Winnie-the-Pooh* book, to our table. Sara thought that Betsy would have plenty to share at future dinners. "Please call me Betsy," she said. "We've been looking forward to your arrival. Can't wait for you to join us for bingo night!"

The waitstaff started distributing the salad plates to the diners. Someone commented that Joseph would not be joining the group for dinner as his daughter had taken him away on a trip. Sara wondered how many of the diners at her table had family that came to take them to dinner or on trips. She hoped that Michael would do that sometimes but knew that he was busy with his job and Marcy, his wife. Sara had few family members and even fewer who lived close to her now.

Dinner was palatable but certainly not what she was used to. When she lived alone she often cooked family favorites and shared the leftovers with her neighbors. It would be quite an adjustment to eat what was prepared instead of what she was hungry for. It was all part of the changes being force-fed to her at the same time that her independence was being ripped away.

The day of transition was coming to a close, but many questions remained. What would the future bring as this new chapter of Sara's life unfolded?

Chapter Two:
Reality Check

childhood decisions

Was this all a bad dream? Could blinking her eyes make her world return to what she wanted it to be? Could she hear the seagulls in the distance calling her name? No. When Sara opened her eyes she was not in her cottage by the sea but instead in the new surroundings she had been introduced to yesterday. It was clean. It was nice. But it was not home.

There was a tap on her door but she ignored it and closed her eyes hoping to return to the life she loved. Return to the cottage by the sea that was her home for decades...the cottage that housed all her memories, both good and bad, but still the memories that were the foundation of her life, now gone. She had outlived her ability to live alone and must now live surrounded by other geriatric adults and be monitored like a two-year-old. She was beginning to understand that it must be true what they say about babies and old people having so much in common. This was labeled unassisted or independent living but it sure didn't feel that way.

Sara drifted back to sleep in an effort to erase the present. Her mind wandered to a long-forgotten memory. She was a young girl, fifteen years of age. She had been tasked with making a monumental decision on the eve of her parents' separation. She must choose which parent she wanted to live with and she chose her father. She had to yank out her American roots and transplant herself in Ireland to be with him. It was not a decision Sara ever regretted but *what if...*

"Come along Sara or we'll be late for church," *Mother called. I love going to church and sharing time with my many friends there. It's a place where I can find peace and acceptance, something that is lacking in my dysfunctional family life.*

My parents are going through an ugly and painful separation with a divorce lurking right around the corner. I want to blot the fighting, name calling and accusations out of my mind but that seems impossible. My two siblings and I are pawns in the marital battles of our parents and it is evident that there will be no real winners. These two adults and three children will never be an intact functional unit again as the unrest within is tearing the very fabric of the family into shreds that can never be repaired.

Because neither parent wants to be responsible for the possible unhappiness of their children by deciding who we'll live with, each of us has to make the choice. Our parents can't share custody because our father will be moving out of the country for work. My brother and sister and I will choose, and our parents and the court will make the final decisions.

I expect my brother Tom to choose our father as they share many activities and interests and they have a special male connection. It makes perfect sense for my teenage brother to choose to live with him especially since it will open up a whole new world for Tom in Ireland. There will be new father/son adventures and experiences Tom won't have if he stays with our mother. It also means that Tom will have to leave behind his friends, teammates and his sweetheart. Tom's decision will be a double-edged sword for him but I feel that he'll ultimately choose our father.

Barbara is the youngest of my siblings and a real Mama's baby. She is eight years old and already an accomplished musician of sorts. She can play the piano by ear and is often the center of attention at church and family gatherings. Barbie, as we call her, is really a child prodigy. She could read first-grade *books when she was three years old and will more than likely graduate from high school before she reaches full puberty. I try not to be jealous of Barbie's wealth of knowledge and God-given musical abilities, but it's often almost impossible for me to make that happen.*

I care a great deal for my younger sister but Barbie is often showered with praise and affection from our parents. I know it's childish of me but I often feel I live in the shadows of my younger sister's intelligence and my older brother's athletic ability. I am average or even maybe a bit above average, but I can never compete with their almost galactic capabilities. I know that Barbie will certainly miss Father but she will definitely choose mother as her resident parent or mother will be chosen for her.

Now I must decide what I am going to say when asked about my decision. I love both my brother and sister and cannot imagine life without either one of them. I also fear what living will be like having only a single parent in my everyday life. We'll no longer have the family outings, vacations and gatherings I grew up with the last fifteen years. There will be empty chairs at the table, unoccupied seats in the car and, worst of all, we will never be a family again in the true sense of the word. My world is crashing around me. I have no control over the chaos and discord. It breaks my heart. Why did this have to happen?

My father is being transferred to Dublin because his company is trying to expand its business there. Although he has said he'd rather stay stateside, he does not have a choice. He'll get in on the ground floor of this American business taking root in Ireland. It's good for him but bad for my family.

My mother, who is a physician, is very busy and we have a full-time au pair, Madylene, to care for us when neither parent is home. Although we all really like Maddy, spending so little time with our parents isn't always a "Father Knows Best" family environment. It's nice having the new big house and all the material items we desire but I am envious of my friends who go home each day to share an evening meal and conversation with both of their parents. That didn't often happen at our house. We never went hungry physically, but we were often hungry emotionally. I missed doing simple, everyday activities with my parents. And now even that was going to get worse. I am miserable and each day is a struggle to put on a happy face. I can't let my parents and siblings see my pain and grief.

I thought long and hard about what I am going to say when it is my turn to choose. I love both my parents but know most of my time will be spent with only one of them. Sure I'll see the other one maybe twice during the school year and several weeks each summer but living like that is difficult to fathom. Too much is changing and too little is staying the same. I like routine. I like normal. I like having an intact family unit. But what I like or want doesn't matter. The decision has been made.

Living with my father in a distant land would certainly be an adventure but the flip side of that "new experiences" coin is the fact that I'll have to adjust to a vast amount of change. There will be new schools, new friends, a new house and the list goes on and on. While I'll have to take Irish lan-

guage classes, I'll still be able to speak my native tongue the majority of the time. I will get exposure to a whole new world, but it comes with a price tag.

Gone will be all my childhood friends, the church that I love to attend, the school that all my classmates since kindergarten attend, my favorite stores and restaurants. All that would cease to exist if I moved to Ireland and started all over there. It's overwhelming. The magnitude of the decision makes my thoughts blur and the room seem to spin.

The day came and we went to the courthouse. My brother and I are scheduled to appear in the courtroom while my sister, Barbie, because of her age, is allowed to do so in the judge's chambers. We will give their testimonies, separately, with both parents, both attorneys and the judge present, but not the other siblings. We won't know the choices the others made until it's over. It's going to be a long, painful, sad day that I hoped would never come.

I paced the hallway as Maddy played a game of Connect Four with Barbie. Maddy will stay at our current home with our mother and anyone who chooses to stay with her. My father will decide if he needs an au pair in Ireland based what happens today. Tom and I are certainly old enough to be left alone but Barbie is not.

Now it's my turn and I am nervous. I love both my parents but I can only choose one of them. It is a difficult and life-changing decision for a teenager to make.

Even though I will miss my father and possibly my older brother, I had to choose my mother. She is a strong role model and an accomplished physician. I often dream of following in her footsteps. Although it will be several years until I graduate from high school and enter college, I have fantasized about being a doctor and using my abilities and education to serve the less fortunate in foreign lands.

If I live with my father in Ireland I don't think I'd have the same likelihood of attending medical school. The United States, on the other hand, could offer me unlimited choices. I said, "I choose to live with my mother," but my eyes, welling with tears, stared at the floor. I knew Mother was overjoyed—I heard a gasp of surprise when I spoke—but I also knew that I had just broken my father's heart. I couldn't bear to see the pain that I knew he felt.

Everything else went like I thought it would. My brother voted to live in Ireland with our father and my younger sister stayed in the states with our mother. The dice had been rolled and the decisions had been made. Neither parent disputed our preferences. In a matter of weeks this decision will be executed and our lives will change forever.

During the first months the changes in our family unit were almost palpable. There wasn't a day that passed in which I didn't think about my father and brother and miss seeing them every day. Their chairs are empty and their voices are absent. It is a very sad time for me.

I enjoy my vacations to Ireland. I anticipate them for months and am never disappointed seeing all the special places my father and brother have come to know and drinking in the Irish culture first hand. My brother graduated from high school in Ireland and attended Mary Immaculate College in Limerick. He met and fell in love with an Irish lassie *and they will be married in the summer. My sister and I will attend the wedding.*

My mother met Daniel, a fellow surgeon, and they married five years after my parents divorced. Although Daniel is a nice man with curly dark hair and a face with the chiseled features of Adonis, he is not my father. When they married, Daniel's two children from his first marriage came to live with us part of the year. It was a definite adjustment for me and Barbie as his two children are boys. It works out the majority of the time but there are certainly bumps in the road.

Sometimes I lay in my bed at night fantasizing about how life could have been if my parents had not divorced, but reality rears its ugly head and chases those thoughts away. I honestly tried to accept the situation but longed to wake up from a really bad dream and have my life return to how it had been before.

I graduate first in my high school class and am admitted to Harvard Medical School. I want to follow in my mother's footsteps but not for monetary reasons; rather for the betterment of those who live in poverty in third-world countries. As soon as I earn my doctorate and serve my residency in pediatrics at Massachusetts General Hospital and Massachusetts General Hospital for Children my plan is to relocate to some remote place and provide medical attention to the suffering masses living with little or no facilities or physicians.

After much research, family discussion and soul searching, I decide to travel to a remote area of Ghana under a medical fellowship. My mother is not supportive of my decision as she fears for my safety and questions my decision to "donate" my time and services instead of choosing a well-paying pediatric position stateside, but I definitely made my mind. This is my calling. I cannot wait to get started.

It's a bone-chilling Massachusetts November day when I board the airplane to start my trip and my new life as a doctor. I am exhilarated by the promise of making a difference to people with so little, and terrified of what to expect on entering a world that's so different from my own. I hope for the best but I fear the worst.

The takeoff is uneventful, and I settle into the window seat to watch the ground disappear below. I try to read the travel guide to Ghana that I had in my carry-on bag but I'm too distracted by my excitement and anxiety over what waits for me upon landing. I'll be living in a remote village in a place I've only seen in pictures. It's frightening but it's also invigorating. I know I made the right decision.

Several hours into the flight we hit some turbulence. We are ordered to return to our seats and fasten our safety belts. I'm not a nervous flyer but the expressions on the faces on the flight attendants worry me. I look out the window. Smoke streams from the engine. Something deep within the aircraft makes a horrible pounding racket. My stomach ties itself into knots. I feel us lose altitude and I pray for a miracle. It all happens so fast. There is screaming and crying and praying. The pounding intensifies. My young life flashes before my eyes and then there is silence…total silence!

Sara opened her eyes and returned to reality. The Parliament Square attendants who had been banging on her door burst into the room. "Sara, are you all right? We thought you might be having an emergency. When you didn't come to the dining room for breakfast, we were worried. Please don't scare us like that again. What's going on?"

Sara shook the remains of the dream from her head. "I am so sorry to worry you but I was simply taking a nap. I don't need to be monitored and checked like a young child. I appreciate your concern but really I am fine. This is my first morning here and I'm not happy about it. I don't need you to add insult to injury by creating a scene at my apartment door. Please leave me alone. I am fine."

Sara vaguely remembered the tapping on the door but she vividly remembered the dream about life with her mother. In reality she had chosen to live with her father. Had she looked back into some time warp and seen what could have been?

She had never had such a dream. It scared her but it also made her think about the decisions she made during the course of her octogenarian life. It was a window into what life could have been if she had chosen a different path. The dream was so vivid, so real, so frightening. Was she losing her sanity? Was this yet another surprise of the aging process? Was it caused by the stress and unhappiness of leaving her cottage by the sea? Was it cause for alarm? Was she having a mental breakdown?

She dressed and went to the dining room but couldn't get the dream out of her head. Would her life have been over when she was twenty-eight if she had chosen to live with her mother when she was fifteen? Could that dream have possibly been true?

It was almost too much to think about. Would this happen again or was it a one-time occurrence? She wanted to call Michael but hesitated because she worried that he might think she was becoming senile. She would keep it to herself for now.

Chapter Three: Acclimation

not to be

A day at Parliament Square flowed easily like sand through an hourglass but Sara felt like each day was much like the day before and tomorrow would mirror today. She had little to look forward to but tried hard to accept her new surroundings and daily routine. She still longed for the ocean breezes and salty smell of the sea.

The aspect of life that she missed the most, however, was her independence. She wondered if others around her felt the same way. Although she attempted to fit in she felt like an outsider. She understood that her adjustment to all the changes would not happen overnight, but she wanted it to feel more like home and less like she was a visitor in what was being *called* her new home. This was not her home. This was a holding tank for those of advanced age and infirmity to wait until their number was called. It was like a lottery but not the kind for which you want to be holding the winning number.

Life was drawing to a close, but the final act was yet to be staged. She wanted to cry most days but called on her inner strength to evaporate the tears as exposing her unhappiness would show her vulnerability and Sara would not allow that.

Although there were many planned activities for the residents each week, many of them didn't appeal to her. She found some contentment just staying in her room with a good book and Penelope on her lap. Her dining companions encouraged her to attend the events and sometimes it was easier to accept the invitation than it was to make excuses for declining. The first activity she agreed to attend was Tuesday-night bingo in the community room. She was not sure what to expect but she told herself it would be fun and remembered Michael's encouragement to get involved and participate.

Jan and Betsy knocked on her door at 6:45. Sara graciously answered the door putting on her best "I can do this" face. Jan entered first and just about knocked Sara to the floor with her effervescent entry and embrace. "Sara," she said, "we are so excited that you accepted our invitation to attend bingo night. I have a feeling deep in my brittle bones that you are going to be a winner. Here, kiss my lucky rabbit's foot. My left knee has been aching all day and that is always a sign of good luck. Bets and I will be your good luck charms. Oh, that reminds me: I have my favorite charm bracelet on tonight. I can tell you a story about each and every charm on it."

Betsy, dressed in her normal wool ensemble and thick head of curls still damp from the shower, followed Jan through the door. "We don't have time for you to talk about all your charms right now," she said. "We'll be late for bingo. Let's get moving before we have to sit in the back of the room away from the cookie table. We don't want Sara to miss out on the cookies."

Sara wished that she could be that excited about bingo night. *Maybe in the coming months?* she silently asked herself. Penelope bolted to the other side of the room and scurried under the rocking chair for protection. She was not used to all this activity or visitors. Sara wished that she could hide under the chair too.

Sara left several lights on for Penelope, grabbed her purse, and the three headed out the door. Jan said they wanted to get there a little early because Celeste and her friends always tried to arrive before them to get the seats closest to the refreshment table. Jan wore her lucky rabbit's foot on a chain around her neck and a top that was so loud you could almost hear her coming. Betsy and Jan had been friends for decades before they both made the decision (or their families made the decision for them) to move to Parliament Square. They even had adjoining rooms on the fourth floor. Sara wished she had a friend to share her life with but for now Penelope would be her best friend.

When they exited the elevator, which had an unusual but not unpleasant smell, they encountered Celeste and her band of refreshment-craving comrades headed for the community center. Jan expressed her displeasure with Celeste and her friends trying to beat them to the room to grab the "best" seats in the house with an eye roll and an audible sigh. It was like being in grade school again but Sara ignored Jan's attitude and struggled to continue feigning interest for bingo. Was this really what her life was going to be like? Ceasing to exist would be better than living like this but that was not currently an option.

Each resident was provided with two bingo cards and a marker and encouraged to find a seat. The staff stocked the refreshment table and the bingo caller waved and greeted the residents. There were five tables with ten chairs placed around each one. Some tables were filling up while others were only partially full or even empty. Jan almost sprinted to the table closest to the refreshment area which had three unoccupied seats. She feverishly motioned for Betsy and Sara to grab the last two seats. The clock on the wall showed five minutes until 7:00. It was almost time for the excitement to start. Sara could hardly contain herself...or could she? Her eyesight might be a bit blurred but her sarcasm remained intact.

The announcer had a couple of upcoming events to broadcast before the games began. Some were met with applause from the residents. There was going to be a trip to a flower show in two weeks, which would be a day-long event. They announced the location of the weekly grocery shopping trip. Since many residents, like Sara, had their own kitchens, the weekly grocery trip gave them an opportunity to stock up. Although most residents frequented the dining room for breakfast and dinner, it was not mandatory. Those who didn't like the entrée of the day or didn't feel like dressing for breakfast or dinner had the option to cook for themselves in their own apartments. Sara remembered how she loved to cook for David during their marriage. That seemed like another lifetime, she thought. How had the years passed so quickly and robbed her of both her youth and her independence?

"Under the B...12...B12." Bingo was underway. The residents hunkered down each one watching two cards as if the winner was going to be awarded a new Rolls-Royce. This was a big event for them. How sad, Sara thought, but who was she to judge others? In several months she may be anticipating this night as much as Jan, Betsy and the rest. Sara marked her cards as the numbers were called and before long the first "Bingo" was called out by Celeste. Jan mumbled something under her breath and the next game began. Celeste won a bag of candy bars and celebrated like she won a new TV. This group was easy to please.

Jan and Betsy kept reminding Sara to watch her cards and hovered over her like a mother bird sitting on her nest of babies. Did they really think Sara couldn't play bingo? After an hour they called the last game of the evening and announced the winner would receive the night's big prize, a gift card for one visit to the Parliament Square hair salon. Much to Sara's surprise she shouted "Bingo" and won the coveted grand prize. Needless to say, Jan and Betsy were very excited. Jan did a geriatric version of the victory dance and loudly sang a couple verses of "We Are the Champions." Betsy cheered her on like she used to when she was a college cheerleader. Sara felt embarrassed as all eyes followed her as she walked up to receive the gift card. Her comfort level with group activities needed work. Hopefully time would make that happen.

Jan and Betsy stayed for refreshments; Sara excused herself and went to the lobby where there was an assortment of thickly padded upholstered furniture and chose a floral-patterned wing chair in the far corner of the room. It was quiet. Everyone was in the community room eating the after-bingo refreshments. Sara rested her head on the back of the chair and closed her eyes. She was overwhelmed with all the changes in her life over the past several weeks. She was doing her best to deal with it all but it was an uphill battle. Sara tried to relax and achieve an inner peace.

Her mind took her to a memory from long ago when she was a teenager. She had just returned to America after living with her father and brother in Ireland. She reunited with a young man she hadn't seen since she was fifteen. Andrew had grown into a handsome college student. They rekindled their friendship and it blossomed into a profound love like Sara had never known.

Their relationship quickly turned physical and in a matter of months Sara was an unmarried and pregnant eighteen-year-old. Her mother was mortified and insisted that Sara and Andrew marry immediately.

After they settled in together Andrew withdrew from college and enlisted with the 3rd Infantry Division. After training he would be stationed in Korea. It was 1953 and the news on TV said that the end of the war was in sight. Sara begged Andrew to stay in college saying that they could live with her mother and step-father until he graduated but he insisted he would take care of his new family without help from others.

Shortly after Andrew shipped out Sara delivered a still-born baby girl and additional complications left Sara unable to conceive again. She was now barren with no child and a husband fighting a war halfway around the world. It was one of Sara's most difficult memories, but *what if...*

"Surprise" they shout as I enter the room. My family and friends are throwing me a shower for the baby who is due in one month. I'm certainly glowing and growing bigger by the day, but internally I am a mixture of excitement and apprehension! Several of my friends advised me that I should put the baby up for adoption, but I just cannot do that. I understand

this event will be life-changing but I feel raising the child is my only option. Andrew and I are going to be good parents even though we are young. Many people have children in their teens.

My friends all put girl and boy names into a hat. It would be nice to know the baby's sex before he or she is born but the mystery makes it more exciting. Inside I am hoping for a little girl, but I know that Andrew wants a son. We will be happy with either as long as the baby is healthy and normal. I pick out names one at a time and read them aloud. Some are contenders while others are humorous at best. I have always loved the name Kathryn; Kate or Katie for short. Andrew left in such a hurry that we hadn't even discussed baby names.

Unfortunately, Andrew would not be home in time to experience the birth first-hand. My younger sister, Barb, offered to be there to hold my hand during delivery but it isn't the same as having the baby's father there with me. I am not as worried about the pain of delivery as I am about giving birth in front of a room full of strangers—doctors, nurses, technicians—without Andrew there to support me. I consider a home birth but my Mother feels that it's too dangerous and insists I have the baby in the hospital.

Many of my childhood friends are at the shower, friends I grew up with and friends I haven't seen in years. Life can change people. Some friends look almost the same as I remember them, but others have grown and changed in many ways. I feel close to some but a lifetime away from others. It's nice that my mother and sister arranged for everyone to attend my shower but I still feel a bit embarrassed about what's happening to my body. I have always been quite thin and extremely fit. Now I am trapped in this large, random gas-expelling, urine-overflowing, rotund body while my friends are still sleek and slender in their cute sundresses and sandals. I can barely even see my feet.

Being pregnant changes your body and your mind. I feel that I'm living in a different world than my single friends whose biggest worry is what color nail polish to use or whether to wear their shoulder-length hair loose or tethered in a fashionable French twist. That was my life until eight months ago. It seems like a lifetime ago as I attempt to escape from the grips of the over-upholstered couch and waddle off to the bathroom.

The baby shower is so much fun and we receive so many nice gifts for our new baby. For the near future, while Andrew is deployed, I am living with my mother and step-father. They have a beautiful home with plenty of space for us.

I do miss my father and brother, neither of whom has returned from Ireland. My father's job became his life-long career there. My brother decided to remain in Ireland because his wife, who is an Irish citizen, refuses to leave. They are both supportive of my decision to marry Andrew and bear his child, but neither is able to return to the US to welcome the baby. I am sure they'll visit as soon as they possibly can.

The last weeks of my pregnancy are difficult. It's hard to sleep and there are never-ending trips to the bathroom. It feels like the baby is tap dancing on my bladder. I miss Andrew more than ever and send him letters every day. He has limited time to corre-

spond but I do receive occasional notes telling me that the war should be over any day and he can't wait to return home to us.

I am at church when my water breaks and the family rush me to the hospital. I deliver a healthy and beautiful baby girl and name her Kathryn Elizabeth. I'm happy but overwhelmed. Only time will tell if the decision I made to keep the baby will turn out to be the best decision for everyone.

Many years later I am elderly and unable to care for myself, alone in my cottage by the sea. Kate and her family insist that I come to live with them. Although I'm afraid that I will be a burden to the family and decline her kind offer several times, Kate takes control and moves me from my cottage to her home, disregarding my concerns. Both Kate and Kirk, her husband, are adamant about me not going to a retirement community to live with strangers, and in all honesty I am thankful they are.

Now I will live out my days in their lovely home with my daughter, my grandchildren and hopefully in the future my great-grandchildren. What a blessing it is to have a daughter who welcomes me into her life with open arms. I wonder what my life would be like if Kate hadn't come along, if I had given her up for adoption, or if she hadn't invited me to live with her when age took away my ability to live alone. I am so lucky to have a daughter like Kate.

Suddenly Sara was literally shaken back to reality when Jan and Betsy loudly arrived in the lobby, bounding over to Sara and telling her all about the shortage of chocolate-chip cookies after bingo. They went into great detail about how they got the last two cookies right before Celeste came to get one.

Jan, in her outside voice, said "I made sure to apologize out loud to Celeste that all the cookies were gone and I gave her my best really sad face while licking the cookie crumbs off my lips. Serves her right because last week I saw her slip several cookies into a sandwich bag for later when she thought no one was watching. Who does that?" Then they were so engulfed in laughter Sara could barely understand them when they told her that Andy laughed so hard at a joke that punch came out of his nose. Betsy attempted to reenact the event using her cup of water but she just made matters worse when she choked and sprayed a barrage of water across the room. These two could be the poster children for the saying *Laughter is the best medicine.*

They were having such a great time. Sara was jealous of their friendship. She was also upset because their loud frivolity had awakened her from her wonderful dream about Kate. If only she could turn back time and change the future. Wouldn't that be wonderful? She closed her eyes in an effort to return to the warmth and safety of her daughter's home and family but it was too late. That moment was not reality, but Jan and Betsy singing "old McDonald had a farm, E I E I O" certainly was.

Would these flashbacks to what could have been continue? Were they something to be concerned about and discuss with a doctor? Would this have happened if she stayed in her cottage by the sea or were they a byproduct of her resistance to change? A stress-induced side-effect of moving to this golden-ager community and having her residential independence compromised? Too much to ponder. She was getting a headache.

Chapter Four:
Resistance

first love

The cloudy gloomy weather mirrored Sara's feelings about her new residence and way of life. The days passed one after another with little to look forward to or get excited about. She remembered hearing her relatives complain about getting older and dealing with an old person's body that appeared out of nowhere one day.

She could deal with the infirmity and the daily aches and pains, but the lack of purpose and the evaporation of her independence were what really hurt. The arthritis and the slowdown in her daily activities were one thing; being monitored and supervised both day and night was another. It was like being a young child again and having your parents constantly checking on your well-being, location and activities.

She understood the employees of Parliament Square were paid to take care of the residents but the bottom line was Sara did not want to be one of those residents. How could she escape the shackles of this incarcerated existence? She rocked on her chair with Penelope on her lap thinking, thinking, thinking about how she could escape.

As Sara prepared to go down to the dining room for dinner she continued to ponder her dilemma. There must be some way she could sneak out. But where would she go? She didn't have a car (which was irrelevant since her driver's license had been revoked over a year ago because of her diminishing eyesight) and there was no public transportation close by. She would have to stow away in someone's vehicle and have them unknowingly transport her away from here. That was what she would do. She would be a stowaway. Maybe the driver of the getaway vehicle would feel sorry for her and help her escape. This plotting and scheming was the most exciting thing she had done since she arrived at Parliament Square.

The dinner conversation was dreadfully boring as usual and the potatoes were overcooked and tepid. No Julia Child wannabes in this kitchen, that was evident. This was the first evening meal at which Joseph, the eighth resident at her table, was in attendance. He had been on a trip with his daughter and her family since Sara moved in and tonight his seat was no longer empty. Joseph was an attractive gentleman with eyes of crystal blue and skin that was darkened from sitting in the sun, probably against his daughter's advice. She felt a cold shiver run down her spine. Where did that come from she wondered?

Maybe he had an octogenarian rebellious spirit and would want to escape with her. What would he think if she asked him to break the shackles of imprisonment with her? No, she certainly could not talk to him about this. She did feel chemistry between them, even at this first breaking of bread, but maybe it was all one-sided.

Joseph was casually dressed with a hint of affluence in his clothing. Nothing specific, but something that Sara found very appealing. The other women at the table seemed to focus on his conversation and presence. He was definitely, as the younger generation put it, the "eye candy" at the table. Maybe being seated at this table had its advantages. At least she wasn't surrounded by women.

"Nice to meet you Sara and so glad you were assigned to our table of seasoned-in-years but youthful-in-spirit dining room companions" Joseph said in a deep authoritarian tone. When they shook hands she felt a flow of warmth through her body that almost scared her and made her blush. "We have shared many meals together at this table and in doing so we have learned deep, dark secrets about each other's past." He winked at the others seated around the table and continued. "Now it is our turn to learn about you as your history unfolds over meatloaf and green beans. It's our mission to verify or dismiss the rumor we heard about you being an exotic dancer when you were younger. We have so much to learn."

When he finished speaking and sat down, everyone at the table applauded and chuckled over his welcoming speech to Sara. There certainly were details of earlier years discussed over dinner together each day but none were either deep or dark. Many were amusing. Others were sad and a bit depressing. Some could be described as embarrassing at best. Stories were often repeated, but no one ever spoke up to say *You told us that story before!*

After dinner Sara continued to devise a plan in her head that would allow her to sneak out. Still not sure how she was going to make it work but somehow it just had to. Then once out of this geriatric prison she would decide her next moves. One step at a time. Her only concern with leaving was what would happen to Penelope. She certainly could not stow away carrying a cat in a carrier and who would take care of her best friend when she was gone? A lot to think about. She was getting a headache.

After dinner some of the residents went to the community room to watch a documentary about the Korean War. That was a sensitive subject for Sara and she declined the invitation to join. She just wanted to go somewhere quiet, away from the others, and work on her escape plan.

Sara returned to her room and perched herself on the well-padded loveseat on the veranda overlooking the constantly maintained gardens. Penelope jumped on Sara's lap and curled into a ball of purring fur. How Sara loved this little kitty that was now her constant companion and best friend. She often initiated conversations with Penelope and spoke for both parties. Was that a sign of senility? No, she had been doing the two-way talks with animals for many years, long before she became an "old" person. Michael used to ask her if she was talking to him sometimes during her exchanges with furry friends.

Sara hated the label of *old* or *elderly* or *senior citizen*. She was a mature woman well past her prime but in no hurry to be pushing up daises. She still had too much to do before her time was up, her number was called, her goose was cooked. And the first task was to break out of this jail.

Maybe she could form a cult of followers who would join her in her escape. No, she was too new to have others she could count on to sign up for duty. Maybe in time but not now. And some of the residents seemed to be comfortable with their life here. They were excited by the weekly activities and upbeat in their attitude and demeanor. Maybe Sara needed to give the experience more time, maybe she would acclimate to life here. Maybe Michael was right, this was where Sara needed to be.

She spent a good part of her life trying to eat well, maintain a healthy weight and exercise only to find the benefit of living longer was not what she expected. Sure she was still alive and breathing but she was not happy or able to live her additional years as she expected. She was not prepared for this confined environment during this phase of her life that they referred to as the "golden years." That expression certainly was not coined by someone her age. There was nothing golden about being her age except maybe some of the fillings in her teeth.

As the sun was setting Sara closed her eyes for a moment. Why had she declined the after-dinner history lesson? The others didn't know the pain that one battle in the war had caused her. It still hurt her deep inside to even think about it. Although so many years had passed since it happened, it still cut her like a knife when she let the memories bubble to the surface. It was one of the saddest times in her life. So unexpected...so devastating...so life-changing.

The battle of Kumsong started on July 14th, 1953. Sara had just lost the baby weeks before and was still recuperating from the difficult delivery when there was a knock on her door on the morning of July 19th. She almost fell to her knees when she saw the two officers. They had come to deliver the news that Andrew had lost his life in the battle of Kumsong on July 14th. The last battle of the war which would end with the Korean Armistice Agreement on July 27, 1953 had taken her precious Andrew.

If only he had remained safe for another two weeks. The war would have been over and he would have returned now to her. How could this be happening? She was not even certain that Andrew had received the news about the loss of the baby. She had written to him about it but had not heard from him since she mailed the letter. Sara so needed his support at this most difficult time and now she not only didn't have his support...she didn't have him! It was one of the lowest times in her life, but *what if...*

> *The Korean War is over and many of the troops are returning stateside to reunite with their families. I am minutes away from feeling the warm, tender, healing embrace of Andrew's arms. The crowd at the train station anxiously awaits the return of their loved ones as the train approaches the station. One by one the soldiers disembark and reunite with family and friends after their long and difficult deployment. I search the crowd hoping to see Andrew's face. When I see him I run to greet him and melt into his arms hoping his presence will erase some of the pain and suffering I am dealing with after losing the baby. He has written to me expressing his sadness that the child we conceived together will not be here to greet him upon his return. Although the baby was unplanned, as was our hasty marriage, we are accepting and optimistic about our married life together. We are young and have many years ahead*

of us. They will be childless years but we could always adopt a child when we're ready.

Andrew and I live with my mother and stepfather until we are able to afford to buy a place of our own. Mother never really accepts Andrew or the fact that I could never grace her with grandchildren. As the years unfold Andrew and I operate a successful restaurant and make a good life for ourselves. Running the business, we are so focused on our careers that we never explore the adoption process and we accept the fact that we will never be parents. We are aunt and uncle to my younger sister Barb's three children and enjoy being involved in their lives as they grow to adulthood. It's not the same as having our own family but we are happy with our life and the success we have worked so hard to achieve.

In moments alone, I often fantasize about how our life's experiences would have been different if Kate had been born healthy. Although we are happy and successful through our married lifetime, I feel that something is missing and that something is our beautiful daughter, Kate. What would she have been like? Would she have had siblings? Would Andrew and I have been good parents? Would we have been so focused and committed to our business and had such success if we had to share our time and energy with a family? All questions with no answers but questions that sometimes woke me from a sound sleep.

Andrew and I travel to many interesting and exotic locations during our marriage. We enjoy exploring new places together. We travel with other couples we befriended over the years and have a wonderful life together in spite of not having a family. We grow old together!

Sara was jolted from her reverie when Penelope leaped from her lap and ran under the rocking chair, startled by a knock on the door. She opened it and found Joseph standing in the hallway. Did he come to the wrong room by mistake? Did he have memory issues? Sara tried to clear her own mind of what her life with Andrew could have been and focus on the situation at hand.

"May I come in?" he asked. Sara reluctantly agreed. Although Joseph appeared to be well-mannered and personable at dinner, she knew nothing about him. Once inside her apartment they sat on the veranda as the sun retreated behind the horizon radiating beautiful shades of orange and red. They marveled at the beautiful evening lights.

Joseph spoke first. "When my wife of fifty-eight years succumbed to cancer, I thought life was over for me. We had been together since we first met at college. She was the only woman I ever truly loved. We raised a family together. We built a business together. We were two bodies sharing one spirit. I could finish her sentences and she could finish mine. It was as if a part of me died when she died. I wanted to leave this world and be with her again in her new one."

Sara empathized with his loss; she felt that way when she lost her precious David years ago. The healing process was slow, painful and difficult. Her friends used to tell her that with time the pain would lessen and to some degree they were correct. The years did heal her soul a bit, but each time a special date rolled around her heart ached for him and their times together.

Last year on his birthday she didn't leave her bed. She wanted to put her head under the covers and pretend David was still with her. If she got up and went to the other rooms his absence cut her like a knife. Being with your soulmate is a wonderful experience until your soulmate is no longer there.

Sara knew that nothing she could say or do could erase the pain of Joseph's loss. That would take time, acceptance and healing on a personal level. Sometimes people never heal after such a loss. Sometimes they do.

They talked for quite some time and Sara enjoyed his company that evening. It was really the first time since she was at Parliament Square that she did not feel like crying and running away. Maybe her plan to escape was silly and would never come to fruition. Sara was so grateful for Joseph. The other residents were friendly, but Sara didn't feel a connection with any of them. She felt differently about Joseph.

When Joseph stood to leave he said, "I apologize for imposing and I hope you weren't offended at dinner when I said you may have been an exotic dancer. It was my attempt at humor. This may sound strange but when I met you at the dinner table, it felt like I was reuniting with an old friend. I know we're not; in fact, we never met before today. I don't want you to think I've lost my marbles or have some disease of the mind, but something just clicked. It's as if we knew each other in another life, our spiritual life paths crossed at some point. I'll stop there before you call security. I know this must sound like a crazy man talking."

Sara replied, "It was no imposition at all and it's nice that you felt comfortable enough to share your personal thoughts and feelings. As far as the spiritual connection, I must confess that I too felt something when we met. Like you said, it was hard to explain but it was there. Please feel free to visit any time you like." Just as Sara opened the door, Deborah walked by and gasped at the sight of Joseph leaving Sara's apartment. They exchanged hellos and Deborah quickly retreated into her apartment. Sara thought to herself that this might provide the other residents some fodder for conversation in the coming days.

As Sara was shutting her apartment door Jan and Betsy skipped by and broke into song. Off they went on their merry way singing "This old man, he plays one...He plays knick knack on my thumb...With a knick knack paddywhack... Give the dog a bone...This old man comes rolling home." Sara smiled. It was wonderful to see two lifelong friends enjoying the evening and their life no matter what the future held for them. They were living it to the fullest while they had the chance.

Probably a good lesson for Sara. The thought of escaping started to fade. She couldn't imagine leaving Penelope behind anyway. Her resistance was weakening. And now she felt a connection with Joseph. Though they had just met, Joseph had sought out Sara's company and felt comfortable enough to share personal moments with her. He was such a handsome man and so vulnerable. Maybe she could help him and he could help her as they both struggled with life's challenges.

Chapter Five: Dependence

early life choices

The first daylight tiptoed through the chintz curtains and cast shadows dipped in morning sunshine on the wall as Penelope softly placed her paw on Sara's arm. Sara had been drifting in and out of reality embracing remnants of her wonderful what if life with Andrew. Penelope's morning routine of reminding Sara that it was time for breakfast quickly jostled her back to reality. She was not on a tropical island basking in the sun with Andrew or on a historical tour of the vineyards in France. She was in her bed at Parliament Square.

Since moving in almost a month ago, Sara had awakened several times without knowing where she was. For a moment it would startle her. Why was she here? Where were all the familiar and comfortable parts of her world that had greeted her every morning for so many years? Where were the pieces that fit together to make her puzzle of life complete? Then the veracity of the situation reared its ugly head and Sara was reminded of the fact that she was living a new chapter of her life. The pages had closed on the prior chapters, never to be reopened.

Independence was highly underrated and taken for granted until it was stolen away and replaced with a life of dependence. Sara thought that losing her independence for even day-to-day events was the most difficult adjustment to make. She heard younger people say things like, "It's for her own good," or "She is much safer now," or the one Sara hated the most, "We think she will be very happy there."

Instead of dressing and going to the dining room for breakfast, Sara decided to have breakfast with Penelope in her apartment. She needed some time alone to contemplate not only her day but also her life. This adjustment wasn't easily, but Michael had worked so hard she wanted to at least give it a chance. In the back of her mind she was still orchestrating her escape and a return to her life outside these walls of confinement.

After showering, Sara caught a glimpse of her naked body in the full-length mirror. Why do they put these mirrors anywhere, let alone in the bathroom, directly across from the shower door? It was like looking onto a fun-house mirror. What used to be a toned, firm and normal-weight body had transformed over the years into a mass of sagging skin comprising ripples and valleys dotted with imperfections that seemed to appear almost overnight. She looked like a connect-the-dots puzzle.

She grabbed her towel and hid her nakedness from the mirror's reflection. The aging process was not kind nor gentle nor pretty. Unless one could afford the transformation of bodily structures and features by a reputable, expensive plastic surgeon; one was doomed to accept the transformation from young to middle-aged to past-your-prime. It was inevitable there would be sagging, there would be wrinkles and there would be the growth of hair in the most curious places all over the body except on the head. It was not a pretty sight!

And then there was the clothing. Dressing like you're in your twenties when you're in your forties is doable under the right circumstances, but dressing like you're in your twenties when you're in your eighties is embarrassing to yourself and everyone around you. She had seen some residents in the hallways who were in dire need of age-appropriate fashion advice.

Sometimes, when Sara looked in the mirror, she wondered who the old person was looking back at her. The years had passed, but internally she still felt pretty much the same way she did when she was younger. How could someone of advanced age not feel mentally old or think old thoughts? She believed that her mind still thought and responded based on a pattern established when she was younger. The worst part about getting older was that no one can see you're still young on the inside.

Although Sara accepted the fact that the sand in her hourglass was much fuller at the bottom than at the top, her thinking didn't always reflect that knowledge. Her thoughts wanted to be ageless. She knew she couldn't do the same physical activities that she could when she was younger. But she wouldn't allow her mind to close the door on abilities and activities that remained possible at a slower pace or lesser intensity.

Thinking she could do nothing more than exist would open the door to complacency and a premature death. She was NOT ready to live her remaining years in that frame of mind and she was NOT ready to check out. She had value. She had spirit. She had *life*.

Sara felt better after giving herself a mental pep talk. Although she was not happy like she was in her cottage by the sea, she began to adjust a bit to her circumstances. The other residents were quite friendly and outgoing. They tried to make her feel at home which was an uphill battle most days. Maybe she needed to give it a chance. What other options did she have?

She had almost decided to give up trying to sneak off the premises because she couldn't leave her sweet Penelope and she certainly couldn't take her along. She was going to see Michael this weekend and she would discuss her concerns with him. He was a good listener and he would have wonderful words of encouragement. Also, in the back of her mind, she was thinking about Joseph's visit and their talk. She wanted to get to know Joseph better.

Sara rested her head on the back of the sofa. It wasn't long before she drifted off to her world of memories and another possible event that could have been. Her thoughts wandered back to the terrible time in her life after she had lost both the baby and her husband, Andrew.

She was eighteen years old and had endured losses that such a young woman should never have to experience. Just a year ago she had been living in Ireland, carefree and ready to begin her life's adventure. Now she was alone after not one but two terrible losses that would leave permanent scars on her heart and soul. It was a difficult time in her life, but *what if...*

I am living with my Mother and stepfather after losing both the baby and Andrew. Mother is supportive and encourages me to apply to medical schools. Becoming a registered nurse or doctor has always been what I wanted to do after graduating from high school.

I am overwhelmed with pain and grief. I feel like I'm having a mental breakdown and some days I can't get dressed or even get out of bed. I'm depressed, but most of all I'm scared and alone. Sure, my mother and stepfather are in the house but they have their own lives. Their focus is on my sister Barbie, as it should be. Barbie is now twelve years old, almost a teenager. She remains a musical prodigy with remarkable talent. My mother is so proud of her and, although she never says so, I know that she is disappointed in me.

I have to get away from my mother's house and that won't happen if I enroll in nursing or medical school which is what Andrew and I had planned for me after the baby was born. But now I have no baby and no Andrew. I am a childless widow at eighteen years of age. Going to school and living with my mother is not an option. I need to distance myself from the pain and suffering, change my focus, but how can I do that?

It comes to me one night as I lay in my bed sad and alone: I will join a convent and live the remainder of my life as a nun in the service of God. What better tribute to the baby and Andrew than for me to live a life of reverence in their memory? I won't have to deal with future romantic relationships and thus forsake my love for Andrew. I won't have to deal with the possibility of adopting someone else's child and forsake the life that lived and died within my womb. Above all else I could honor their memory by funneling my grief and sadness into vows of obedience and chastity. This life choice would show that I accept my bereavement and that I am able to find solace in serving a higher power.

I explore convents around New England and discuss the options with my priest. We review the many pros and cons of entering the convent and the lengthy process of transitioning from Christian laywoman to a Cistercian nun living under the vows of poverty, chastity and obedience. It's a life-changing decision but I feel it is the one that best fits my situation and mindset. I visit several convents to explore the focus of each and the community each convent serves and supports. I've always been interested in nursing or helping the elderly and I hope to find an order that will let me do that.

Mother is very much against it. She feels that I'm making this decision in haste because of my current depression and anxiety. She thinks that I should enroll in a nursing school, possibly even enter the field of medicine, and give myself some time to acclimate to the recent tragic events. I'm only eigh-

teen. My life has just begun. I decide, in spite of my mother's disapproval, or maybe in a defiant effort to express my independence, that I will initiate the process to enter the convent and begin a life of sacrifice and commitment. I will serve the Lord and show my mother that I am old enough to make my own decisions.

The sisters at Mount St. Mary's Abbey are warm and welcoming when I visit. The path to becoming a Cistercian nun is a gradual process that progresses through several well-defined stages. The first step is to visit the convent for a monastic weekend. Through the years I progress through postulancy, novitiate, monasticate and finally take the vows to become a Cistercian nun. After eight years, at the age of twenty-six, I take the vows and commit my life to the service of God as a disciple of Christ.

My life is filled with happiness as I am able to help others while working alongside my sisters feeling the warmth of God's love and compassion every day. I eventually learn to accept the losses I incurred prior to coming to the Abbey knowing that my life's path would have been much different without them. I would never have become a sister of God. I would never know this totally committed lifestyle or feel the lifelong love of my sisters in faith.

I will never be alone because I will be allowed to grow old at the abbey being loved and cared for by others. I will never be told I am being moved to a place where I would live out my remaining years among strangers. I will never be robbed of my independence. This has been a wonderful life choice and I believe my mother came to accept it. She never admitted it, but I felt it in my heart.

Sara abruptly returned to reality when she realized some-one was standing over her asking her repeatedly if she was all right. She opened her eyes just enough to see Cindy's face with its overabundance of cosmetics looking down on her. Cindy was one of the staff members who kept tabs on the residents. She was about six feet tall with billows of auburn hair fram-ing her clown-like face. Someone needed to show her how to apply make-up without making herself look like Tammy Faye Bakker.

Sara always wore a minimal amount of make-up because she felt it made a woman look like a mannequin if applied in excess. A little mascara, blush and a colorful lipstick was all. She had noticed that some of the residents tried to hide their wrinkles by filling the creases and ridges with liquid make-up and lots of it. It looked like they had smeared pancake batter on their faces. Is that why some foundations that you apply wet are called pancake makeup?

Sara sat straight up and scolded "You scared years off my life, which at my age could have put me in an early grave. You could have given me a heart attack. Why are you in my room? I am going to have a deadbolt installed on the inside of my door so you people stop invading my privacy. It's a good thing you didn't catch my lover and me in a compromising position. That is one visual you would not soon forget!"

Cindy audibly gasped and then chuckled a little as she must have pictured the scene in her mind. "Sara," she said, "we were worried about you when you didn't come to breakfast or lunch. I knocked on your door several times. I was concerned that something had happened so I used my master key to open the door." Another affront to her privacy, Sara thought but didn't verbalize. She understood that the staff was paid to watch over the residents, but she didn't have like it.

Sara remembered times when she wouldn't leave her cottage for days and no one even noticed. This was another casualty in her transition from living independently to living a life of dependence. Over a lifetime, moving from one phase of life to another was filled with anticipation, excitement and sometimes fear of the unknown. Moving from adulthood to senior-citizen status replaced the anticipation and excitement with one-hundred-percent fear of the unknown. It seemed there was little to look forward to and much to fear.

Joseph walked by her door and asked if anything was wrong. Cindy replied, "All is well. Sara was simply taking a nap." Little did Cindy know that Sara had been deep into a *what if* moment that she wanted to savor a bit longer.

Although Sara had decided against joining the convent after her mother enrolled her in nursing school, she often wondered what her life would have been like had she chosen that path. Unfortunately, that is all she could do was wonder because there was no way of going back and having a do-over. Life gives us many choices. Sometimes we make bad choices for good reasons. Sometimes we make good choices for all the wrong reasons. And sometimes we make good choices for all the right reasons.

Having the ability to determine the best choices during our lifetime is sometimes learned early in life but more often it takes difficult experiences and challenges to teach us how to make the best choices. *Live and learn*, as the saying goes. Unfortunately, it's usually difficult, if not impossible, to go back and reverse choices made along the way.

Sara was at Parliament Square based on choices she had made during her lifetime. What was done was done and now Sara could continue to feel sorry for herself or she could accept this final phase of her life with tolerance and dignity. She was curious about the trips back in time she was having since her departure from the cottage by the sea. Were they a result of her unhappiness and feeling of displacement? Would they continue? Should she share them with a medical professional?

Joseph peeked inside and asked "Sara, may I join you for a while?" Joseph suggested that they sit on the veranda a bit to enjoy the afternoon sun as his apartment was on the east side of the building and the sun had already moved past his windows. Sara thought that was a good idea and invited Joseph to come in and sit with her. Cindy encouraged Sara to come to the dining room for the evening meal since she had probably not eaten much, having been alone in her apartment most of the day. Sara agreed. Cindy said as she exited, "Sara, I won't barge in on you again today—wink, wink," and left, shutting the door behind her. Sara could hear Cindy laughing in the hallway, Joseph clearly not grasping the inside joke.

They sat in silence for quite some time. They were comfortable sitting on the veranda enjoying the warm afternoon sun together. Joseph spoke first. "Sara, I am a lonely and unhappy man since losing my wife. It's so difficult to get up each morning and face the day alone. I know there are plenty of people here at Parliament Square, but they can never replace what Theresa and I had all of our years together."

Sara felt truly sorry for Joseph. She could see the depth of pain and loss in his beautiful sad blue eyes. She reached for his hand and gave it a strong squeeze. "I also lost my spouse after many years of marriage. At first the days were endless and the nights were intolerable. I truly thought I might go mad. The pain was unbearable. I struggled for months and after some time the pain grew less intense and I was able to return to doing some of the things David and I had always done together. I still thought of him every day and missed him the most at dinner and during the evenings when we used to always share time together. Eating dinner alone was the worst. Friends would invite me to join them for meals and events but I declined for many months. I didn't want to be the wet blanket in the group. They understood, but they kept inviting me until finally I was able to reenter the world of the living.

It was difficult, I am not going to tell you that it wasn't, but it was doable."

Joseph said, "After my wife passed, one of my three daughters, Allison, invited me to come live with her family. I felt that would be an imposition and although I truly appreciated her offer I would feel like an intruder. She's married with two children in college. It was time for her to enjoy life with her husband not time to cater to an old man who was anything but the best company. Instead I decided to move to Parliament Square. Allison insisted that I join them on a vacation to take my focus off the loss of her mother and my wife of fifty-eight years. The vacation was nice but it didn't fill the hole in my heart left by Theresa. I don't think anything will ever be able to fill that hole."

The time passed quickly. It was easy for Sara to spend time with Joseph. This was the first time since arriving here that she felt connected to someone. She didn't feel all alone. Maybe this would be a turning point. Maybe she could empathize so well with Joseph because she remembered the pain and despair she felt after losing her spouse, her soulmate and her best friend. The loss was something difficult to understand unless you had experienced it yourself.

Friends told Sara, when she was mourning the loss of David, that they knew how she felt. They tried to help her through the difficult grieving process. Although everyone understands that life will end for each and every one of us, we are seldom ready to arrive at that final destination. When we do leave this world, it's those we leave behind who feel the loss and endure the suffering. We are in a much, much better place. We have to remind ourselves of that in an effort to rise above our loss and again become a contributing member of society. However, that is so much more easily said than done.

Chapter Six: Affirmation

career options

The day finally arrived for the much awaited visit from Michael. He apologized several times for not coming sooner but he traveled a lot for his job and it was impossible to dedicate time for a nice visit with his aunt until today. He promised that they would spend the bulk of the day together doing whatever Sara wished, although he made it quite clear that excluded packing her bags and returning to the cottage by the sea. Connecting with Joseph over the past several days had lessened her desire to return to the cottage but hadn't totally erased her innermost longing to do so.

Sara wanted to look her best for Michael so she scoured her closet for something stylish but not revealing (like there was anything worth revealing), something conservative but not matronly, something that would make her feel pretty and younger than her age. Did clothing even exist that met all those requirements?

She tried on several combinations and finally decided on her favorite red cashmere sweater and a tailored pair of black slacks that provided the optical illusion of a shapely figure. She had learned as she grew older that black clothing was her friend. It seemed to minimize size and enhance shape. Sara accepted the fact that she no longer had the body of a young or even a middle-aged woman.

Another disadvantage of aging: Gravity takes over and the result was not often pretty. The use of supportive undergarments did help minimize the damage but with it came the uncomfortable side effect of the inability to take a deep breath. Lift and support were good, compression and oxygen deprivation were not. Every woman had to learn her limit which was a trial and error process.

Sara sat in front of her dressing-table mirror and lightly applied her blush, mascara and lipstick. She didn't want to overdo it but she also didn't want to look cadaverously pale. She imagined Cindy with her overabundance of makeup and brightly colored lip gloss. It was definitely over the top and Sara didn't want in any way to go that route.

David didn't like Sara wearing much makeup. He always told her that it hid her natural beauty. How she wished David were still alive and with her. She thought of him often even though she had lost him five years ago. He was her soulmate, her best friend and her pillar of strength when life was challenging. Her heart ached, actually physically hurt, when she thought about him. Maybe she wasn't the best resource to counsel Joseph in his grieving process. Or maybe she was exactly the right person.

Sara went to the dining room for breakfast. She was glad to see Joseph at the table along with the others. Although they sat with the same group of residents at the same table for every meal they didn't have assigned seats. Sara thought that was a good plan because it gave everyone a chance to talk with different people.

She did notice that Betsy and Jan often chose seats next to each other; in fact, some days they told other residents the seat next to them was occupied even when no one was sitting in it. Jim was happy to sit next to anyone and seemed to have a story, a joke or an opinion to share with whoever sat on either side of him at the table. Jim had been in sales so he had the ability to strike up a conversation with just about anyone. The others sometimes joked in his absence that he must have been vaccinated with a phonograph needle because he was so liberal with conversation.

Mary and Deborah were the quietest table companions. Mary looked older than her years. Apparently, she had been a sun worshipper prior to the invention of sunscreen. Some alligators had softer less wrinkled skin. She often dressed in dark colors which accentuated her leathery hide. Mary was nice but very private. She seldom discussed her family or activities and kept pretty much to herself, at least at mealtime.

Deborah was also not much of a talker but she was able to express her feelings through her actions and facial expressions. She was the queen of the eye-roll. Her attitude and overall presence made it clear to the others that she was above the rest of them in wealth and heritage.

Sara felt Deborah thought that Parliament Square was below her social ranking. However, her family had chosen it for her so she was here whether she liked it or not. Pam, the remaining tablemate, was pleasant and almost child-like at times. She didn't appear to be stricken with dementia or mental incapacity; she just lived in a simpler world than the rest of them did. *Good for her,* thought Sara. Maybe she knows the secret to being upbeat and happy no matter her age or situation.

The breakfast conversation often comprised a recap of the residents previous night's activities including number of bathroom visits, strange noises, room temperature (too hot, too cold) and weather-related items. It was quite exciting!

After breakfast, the residents were informed of the activities planned for the day by the vivacious, young Energizer Bunny-like social director, Linda. She was a petite young woman who no doubt had been a cheerleader. If not, she had missed her calling. She was always upbeat and radiated enthusiasm.

Linda announced in her outside voice, "This is going to be a tremendous day. In addition to the weekly grocery store trip, we have an afternoon mini-golf excursion planned for all you sport enthusiasts. If that isn't exciting enough, wait: There's more! On the trip back from golfing, we'll stop for soft-serve ice cream in a dozen different flavors. Think about it...twelve choices for your swirled cone. Is this going to be a red-letter day or what??"

Sara wondered if she had ever been like Linda when she was younger. Not that she could remember, but the brain cells didn't always cooperate when diving into the memory pool.

That pool used to be eight feet deep but it was now more like a wading pool. The information was there. It just refused to be recalled at will, if at all.

Although the weekly trip to the grocery store might have been a choice this week for Sara since she was running low on a couple of items, today was her day with Michael. She would have to defer until next week's shopping excursion. Sara returned to her room after breakfast, used the bathroom (always a good idea even if it didn't seem to be necessary at the moment) and touched up her lipstick.

She glanced at herself in the previously unfriendly full-length mirror and what she saw was a woman of years dressed appropriately with the correct amount of make-up and maybe just maybe a glimmer of positivity. She looked forward to her day with Michael.

Sara said goodbye to Penelope, grabbed her purse and left her apartment. She was meeting Michael in the lobby at 10:00 and it was 9:45. Promptness was not one of her most valued traits. She remembered how David was always ready early. He would tell her events were scheduled fifteen minutes earlier than they actually were in an effort to keep her on time.

Sometimes it worked, sometimes it didn't. She remembered David waiting in the car (not always patiently) for her to shut the front door and join him. Sara would always smile and say something humorous to divert him from her tardiness. Like setting the scheduled event time ahead for Sara, Sara's attempt to make David forget her tardiness sometimes worked and sometimes it didn't.

As the elevator door opened Jan and Betsy appeared and greeted Sara with a burst of laughter that was almost contagious. "Can you believe there'll be twelve varieties of soft ice cream for us to choose? I don't know how I'll be able to make a decision," Jan announced.

Betsy replied, "Maybe they'll have samples. I just love free samples." Jan was bedecked in a full-length skirt of both fabric and pattern Sara had never seen before. It was a colorful shiny sateen material dotted with brushed raised wool-like sections. It certainly was one of a kind! She was not sure exactly what the pattern was, but it almost appeared to have eyes that followed her as she entered the elevator.

Betsy wore only two layers of woolen clothing which was less than normal. Almost in unison they asked what Sara's plans were for the day. She told them that her nephew, Michael, was coming to spend the day with her. She wasn't sure what the plans were but she knew that it would be something away from Parliament Square, which was music to her ears. When they reached the lobby Jan and Betsy hurried off to the excursion van. "We'll bring you a menu from the ice cream place so you can see the twelve flavors you missed. Have a great time with your niece," Jan hollered.

"It's my nephew," Sara replied, but the dynamic duo was already out of earshot.

Sara seated herself on one of the floral sofas in the lobby and focused on the door waiting for Michael to appear. She was a couple of minutes early which would have made David very happy. She fidgeted a bit. She was anxious to spend some time with Michael away from this place where she still felt more like a visitor than a resident.

It had only been a month since Sara moved in so she was still in a transitional phase hoping to progress to an acceptance phase in the coming months or, better yet, have Michael tell her he changed his mind and she could return to her cottage by the sea. But she knew that this was a pipe dream. The sooner she could accept moving to Parliament Square as the final chapter in her life, the better off she would be.

Sara noticed some activity outside and Emily, one of the registered nurses, hurried in. Someone had fallen and needed immediate medical attention. Emily ran back to assist the injured resident and the woman at the front desk called 911.

There was nothing unusual about visits from emergency vehicles. Sara had chatted a bit with Emily when she first arrived and told her about her decades working as an RN and her mother's career as a pediatric physician. David used to tell Sara he loved having his own personal nurse available to him twenty-four-seven.

Shortly after 10:00 one of the staff members approached Sara. "Michael called. He's caught in traffic. He hopes to arrive around 11:00 if all goes well. You can return to your room if you want and we'll call you when he gets here. Or you can sit in the lobby and wait."

Sara decided that she was quite comfortable in the lobby and would wait for him there. She did decide to move to another sofa away from the entrance and the bustle of people coming and going. Yes, this was a nice restful location. Sara imagined where Michael might be taking her today and before long she floated back into another *what if* moment in time...

"Mother," I said emphatically, "I do not want to become a doctor. I want to go to nursing school NOT medical school!"

My mother replied, "You are a very smart and focused young woman; you have the ability to become a doctor. Why would you want to settle for being a nurse when you can go to medical school to be a doctor like me?" My mother and I never agreed on my career aspirations. I saw the long hours and challenging schedule take their toll on my mother and our family life while I was growing up. That had been part of the reason I decided to go live with my father when given the opportunity. It seemed to me that my mother was never there for many of the important-to-me events while I was growing up.

Other parents sat on the bleachers while their children performed, but more often than not my parents were absent. Sometimes my father would make an effort to attend but he was more interested in Barbie's recitals or Tom's sports.

My debate team, scouting, and science fair events were often overlooked. As the middle child and the one with no special talents or athletic abilities. I often felt neglected and forgotten. Add to that my parents' work schedule and you have the middle child syndrome. The eldest is the leader. The youngest is the baby. The middle child is forgotten with no real place in the family order.

Add the middle child syndrome to losing the baby and Andrew and you get a depressed and unhappy young woman. After what seemed like an eternity but was really only about a year filled with individual counseling sessions, group grief meetings and family support gatherings, I decide to enroll in a community college with a liberal arts major.

Before choosing a college away from home (and my comfort zone), I want to test the waters by enrolling locally and commuting to classes. The first couple of weeks are difficult. I feel like I'm different from the other students and decades older than they are.

I complete my bachelor's degree with highest honors and am accepted by Boston University's School of Medicine. I'm still not certain this is the correct path for me but my mother encourages me and offers to pay for my college and medical school costs, so I decide to enroll.

It's going to be a long process. I must complete another year of pre-med classes followed by four years of medical school classes. From there I can apply for a one-year internship in order to earn a general medical license to practice medicine. If I choose any medical specialty, I must then complete from three to seven years of residency to practice that specialty. My mother is a pediatrician and wants me to join her practice upon graduation.

The years go by and I am granted residency in pediatrics. My mother is elated. I'm excited but understand I still have much work to do before I can actually follow in my mother's footsteps. During my residency I meet another resident named Daniel. We become good friends but can find little time to kindle a romantic relationship amid our hectic schedules. It's kind of sad because I see many of the same qualities in Daniel that I saw in Andrew.

Maybe I'll never marry again and instead make my career my life. I'll be a successful career woman with nieces and nephews to spoil but no children of my own. I'll be a wonderful aunt but never have the opportunity to be a fantastic mother.

My mother is delighted that I've chosen her medical specialty and upon officially becoming a pediatric doctor I add my name to the other physicians who work at her practice. I love working with the children and often wonder what Kate would have been like. She would have been twelve years old now, almost a teenager. Maybe if she had lived I would never have chosen medicine since college, medical school and my residency would have been a difficult journey for a single mother. Too many maybes.

ELAINE C. BAUMBACH

Because my life is so hectic I put the thought of adopting a child on the back burner. Maybe I'll meet Mr. Right and he'll sweep me off my feet and want to adopt a dozen children. Or maybe I'll live a singular life as a successful pediatric physician and grow old alone.

Sara was gently awakened by Michael as he sat next to her on the floral sofa and softly patted her hand. "What are you dreaming about?" he asked.

"I've been having *Through the Looking Glass* moments since I arrived at Parliament Square. They show me what might have been if I'd made other choices in my life. They aren't scary, but they're certainly thought provoking. Do you think they could be trying to tell me something? They seem so real, but none of them ever really happened. They *could* have happened though, if circumstances had been different. They're *what if* moments."

Michael looked at her as if she had two heads. "What are you talking about, Aunt Sara?" he asked. "Have they given you new medications? I'll check with the staff to see if something has changed that could be causing this. But for now we're off to enjoy our day together!"

Michael escorted Sara through the front door to his beautiful red Porsche. This was the one extravagance that he afforded himself. He opened the passenger door for Sara and she tried to get in gracefully although the seat was quite low. Once she was comfortably inside, Michael gently closed the door and got into the driver's seat.

The day was beautiful with plentiful sunshine and not a cloud in the sky. The motor engaged and they were off, leaving Parliament Square in the distance. Even if she was not independent enough to drive the car she was independent enough to get away from the watchful eyes of the staff with Michael.

64

She felt a shiver run down her spine as the car sped onto the freeway and her day of adventure began.

The first stop was the local farmer's market. They strolled the many aisles commenting on the numerous items available for sale. From time to time they would stop and sit on the benches to watch the people go by, look over their purchases or simply take a rest. The market was quite large and offered a variety of luncheon choices. After some time and discussion they decided on Chinese cuisine and a big cinnamon pretzel with lots of sugar for dessert.

They found a lovely table by a fountain and shared their food until every bite was consumed. "Michael," Sara said, "let's play our people-watching game like we used to do years ago. You remember, we'd choose a person walking by and then we'd each give that person a name and an occupation. You go first."

Michael selected a nicely dressed young woman with long, blonde hair and a small tattoo on her right wrist. "I say this is Cecilia who owns a very popular B&B with her husband Max," he said.

Sara singled out a seasoned gentleman with a well-maintained beard, nicely tanned and dressed in khaki shorts and an animal print short-sleeved shirt. "I say this is Nathaniel who resides with his wife of fifty years, Maxine and an assortment of cats and dogs on the beach."

Michael and Sara both laughed. "This was fun," Michael said, "but we have to move along or we won't be able to get everything done I have planned."

This was much like the old days when Sara would take Michael to the market with her shopping. Except this time the tables were turned and Michael was taking Sara to the market. Time changes many things. Some things change for the better, some do not. The old saying that you have to take the good with the bad certainly applied. The good was being able to come to the market. The bad was not being able to come to the market independently.

The second stop was to the cemetery to put some flowers Sara had picked up at the market on David's gravesite. She used to come every week with fresh flowers and hold a one-sided conversation with David. She would tell him about the weather, what book she was reading, and of course she would tell him about Penelope. David was not really a cat person; he would rather have a dog, but he grew to love Penelope.

Sara felt that David could see Penelope as he watched over Sara from above and sometimes, when Penelope stared into the distance, she felt the kitty could sense David's spirit in the room. Her friends sometimes asked her if visiting the cemetery so often depressed her and she would tell them definitely not. She felt as if she could communicate in spirit with David during her visits. They actually made her feel better and more at peace with her loss.

As the months and years passed, her visits became less frequent. Now that she could no longer drive to the cemetery, the visits would only happen when Michael or someone else brought her there, which wasn't often. "David," she said. "I cannot visit you as often as I used to do. I sold our beach house and moved. It's very hard but I'm hoping to adjust and make it work. I know that you'll understand. I still miss you terribly and long for the day when I'll be with you again. Until then, I love you to the moon and back."

Their third and final stop was at a lovely restaurant where Michael and Sara had dinner. It was a beautiful warm evening and they chose to eat on the outside patio. Colorful lights adorned the trees. The waitstaff was well trained and friendly.

Their waitress was named Kathryn. How ironic on this lovely evening to have a waitress with the name of the child she had lost. Michael was afraid that would upset Aunt Sara but she put his fears to rest. She said that she had met numerous women with that name and that it was a beautiful name. She was glad their waitress was named Kathryn.

It was a memorable night. The dinner was delicious, the company was wonderful and Sara wanted the way she felt to last forever.

As they drove back to Parliament Square Sara went over the day's activities in her mind. It had been wonderful. She had been anticipating this day for weeks and it had certainly lived up to everything she expected and more. Sara hoped that she and Michael would have many more days like this in the future.

Although Sara had no children of her own, Michael was almost like a son to her. They had been very close since he was a young boy and their relationship grew through the years. His mother, Barbara, was often too busy to attend Michael's events but Sara had always been there to support him. Although Sara and Barbara never had a close sisterly relationship, maybe because of the difference in their ages, Barbara had always encouraged Michael to spend time with Sara. Since Barbara's death the connection between Sara and Michael had grown even stronger. Sara was so glad to have Michael in her life. In many ways he was more like a son to her than a nephew.

Michael came around to Sara's side of the car and helped her out of the car and into the building. They said their good-byes, hugged and Michael was off. It had been a truly lovely day.

Several residents waved as Sara entered the building. She spotted Joseph at the table playing cards with three of his female friends. It made her feel strange. Why? Then she remembered what it was: jealousy. She was jealous that Joseph was playing cards with the other women. My goodness, it had been a long, long time since that emotion had made an appearance. Very interesting. Very interesting indeed.

Chapter Seven:
Flirtation

relocation

Sara felt her face flush as she boarded the elevator. Was she blushing? How could her body embarrass her in public with this unsubstantiated show of emotion? She didn't know anything about Joseph except the little he had shared with her when they sat and talked on the veranda. It had been a very long time since a man had piqued her interest. Maybe it was the two glasses of wine she had at dinner with Michael that caused her to feel this way. Yes, that was it. A good night's sleep and this would be just a fleeting memory.

Sara slept well after her wonderful, busy day with Michael. She awoke to the sound of rain beating on the roof. She liked to lie in bed and listen to its cadenced beating on the roof. It reminded her of the rhythmic lapping of the ocean she listened to for so many years at the cottage. It was a calming sound and if not for Penelope's encouragement to get up and be fed, Sara might have stayed there until lunchtime drifting in and out of consciousness.

After feeding Penelope, making coffee and completing her morning routine, Sara wondered what she would do with her day. She was certain there were events Linda had organized. Maybe it was time to participate in a group activity instead of spending the day reading or watching old movies on television. Michael had encouraged her to actively participate so she'd feel more like a member of the community instead of an outsider. He told her she should try to make new friends by attending group activities and becoming involved.

She was still a bit hesitant, but she did understand that you get out of life what you put into it. If she stayed cooped up in her room keeping to herself there would be little chance of fitting in and making this her home. Although she still found it hard to accept the fact that she lived here now and not at her cottage by the sea, it was time to explore the possibilities and make the best of it.

She didn't want to become a grumpy old woman who wasted the last years of her life being lonely and miserable out of defiance. She didn't skip desserts, take classes at the gym and live a healthy lifestyle when she was younger so she could spend the extra years wallowing in self-pity and despair. No, she would start making an effort today. She would make Michael proud.

She showered and dressed and headed for the lobby to review the activities posted on the bulletin board. Maybe there was something that would spark some interest.

As she looked over the possibilities, Linda bounded over on kangaroo feet telling Sara how excited she was to see her thinking about an event. Sara explained that she was just looking and not sure if or what she may want to do.

She missed the early morning stretch class, and the chair Zumba (how was that even possible?) was already in session. The next item caught her eye: Volunteers were needed in the daycare center on Wednesday and Friday mornings.

Parliament Square had an onsite daycare center. It was a win-win situation for the retirement village. It offered an enjoyable, productive activity for the residents while providing an additional source of income for Parliament Square. It was run by licensed facilitators but residents were used as helpers. They read stories, assisted with snack time and filled in as needed with daily activities. This sounded like an opportunity for Sara to connect with youth which would definitely be a breath of fresh air in this golden-ager establishment.

Sara pondered this as she continued reviewing the afternoon activities. The pinochle game sounded too sedentary and the crochet class was a definite no. She had never been one to sew, knit, crochet or quilt.

She chuckled to herself as she remembered the result of her only attempt to knit. She had made a sweater vest for David which ended up having a U-neck, not a V-neck, and armholes of two different sizes. He used to humor her by wearing it but only around the house, never out in public. It was David's inside sweater and their inside joke. Sara kept the sweater after he passed to remind her of him and his wonderful sense of humor. They had enjoyed so many marvelous years together.

The afternoon outing to a local miniature golf range caught her eye. Sara had been quite the golfer in her day, although someone did not have to be a good golfer to play miniature golf. The rain had stopped, it was a beautiful September day and this would give her the opportunity to get some fresh air and enjoy being outside for a while. The trip was scheduled for 1:00.

When she told Linda that she would like to get her name on the list for miniature golf, Linda celebrated like she had won the lottery. For a moment Sara feared that she might do handsprings across the lobby. She'd never seen an adult get so excited about miniature golf.

Sara turned toward the dining room and met Joseph on his way to lunch. "How did your day with Michael go? It was such beautiful weather. You must have enjoyed being away from here for the day."

"Yes, I had a wonderful day." Sara replied. "We went to the farmer's market for lunch, then we visited David's final resting place and wrapped up the day with a wonderful dinner together. It was so nice to get away. I almost wished I didn't have to return and Michael would drive me back to my cottage, but of course I'm still here."

When they arrived at the dining room several of their tablemates were already seated. Joseph pulled out a chair for Sara and took the empty seat next to her. Again there were feelings that she had all but forgotten over the past five years since losing David. It wasn't jealousy like last night. These feelings were difficult to put into words and it was definitely both her mind and body speaking to her. It was not a lustful or physical attraction but rather a warm rush of emotion that took her by surprise.

Since losing David she'd had several gentleman friends. Nothing ever developed because they really were only friends, nothing else; someone to share a nice dinner with or someone to laugh with at a funny movie or someone to simply sit with by the ocean, soaking in the afternoon sun. Sometimes her friends would ask her why she even wanted to be involved with another man at her age. She would reply that love was ageless and not limited to the young but to the young at heart, which anyone can be no matter what their actual age. Companionship at an advanced age was much different than it was for younger generations. It hinges on friendship and camaraderie rather than physical needs and desires.

Lunch was optional for the residents and Sara only came to the dining room at noontime once or twice a week. The menu today included grilled cheese and tomato soup. For those who didn't like the day's offering, there was always a ham-and-cheese sandwich or a chef's salad.

Sara loved grilled cheese with bread-and-butter pickle slices. Much to her surprise, Joseph spoke up and said "I eat my grilled cheese sandwiches that way too. You're the only person I have ever met who likes melted cheese and pickle slices. Maybe we're grilled cheese soulmates?"

That started a conversation about possible permutations of the traditional naked cheese-only grilled cheese sandwich. Jan shared "I love to put a handful of crushed potato chips in my melted cheese. It can be a bit messy, but it adds a nice crunch to the sandwich." Sara thought she saw an eye-roll from Deborah. Jim went into a five-minute lecture about how to make the perfect grilled cheese sandwich. It was like when someone asks you the time and you tell them how to build a clock. The group listened attentively or maybe more politely as he described the process in great detail leaving nothing to the imagination.

Sara asked, "Have any of you volunteered at the child-care center? I'm thinking about signing up but I'm not sure what's involved. Children can be such fun."

Jan and Betsy spoke up in unison saying that they had volunteered and loved the experience. "The children were so cute, happy and eager to learn. It was uplifting to spend a couple hours during the day with them soaking up their enthusiasm. It's so different from the normal, depressing, too-much-free-time-on-our-hands days here. But be prepared because it can be quite exhausting, not to mention messy."

Sara thought the more she got involved the less time she'd have to dwell on her self-pity and dislike of living here. Like Michael told her, she had to make an effort to get involved and to fit in. She decided to sign up to help at the child-care center and maybe try another bingo night. She was also going to schedule an appointment at the beauty shop to use the free visit voucher she won the last time she played bingo.

After lunch Sara went back to her apartment to grab a sweater for the miniature golf outing. The September weather was nice but being in the Northeast means that there's sometimes a chill in the air. Penelope greeted her at the door.

Sara sat for a minute and Penelope jumped on her lap, purring loudly. Her chair was so comfortable, her apartment so peaceful. Maybe she would skip the outing and stay in her apartment with Penelope. A little voice in her head told her to grab the sweater and hurry down to the van. She obeyed that voice and headed for the lobby.

Sara smiled when she boarded the bus and saw Joseph seated in the front. Jim sat next to him and they appeared to be in animated conversation. She overheard something about gun control as she passed their seats and sat several rows back next to a woman she had seen but never met.

73

They introduced themselves and Sara discovered her name was Jean. During the fifteen-minute trip she learned much about Jean. Maybe too much! Jean confided that she had her eye on Joseph. He was such a nice, caring man who recently lost his wife. "Men are most vulnerable soon after becoming widowed," she said. "They need a shoulder to lean on and I am more than willing to provide that shoulder. Then I'm going to reel him in and make him mine. Have you seen his blue eyes and tanned body? I want a piece of that action!" Once again the green-eyed monster flared up deep within Sara. She couldn't believe that her body was once again causing her to feel this way. Seriously, what was going on?

The miniature golf was fun and provided time outdoors to enjoy the fall weather before the cold, dark New England winter arrived. Sara had considered moving to a more temperate climate when she was younger but decided she didn't want to leave her family and friends in the four-season area of Massachusetts. This was where she grew up and where the majority of her remaining relatives resided.

Her brother Tom still lived in Ireland with his wife, children and grandchildren. On the bus ride back to Parliament Square Sara closed her eyes and shut out the conversation, going on around her. Before long she was transported into another *what if* moment. She returned to a time soon after she graduated from college and started her career as a registered nurse...

I'm not happy about working the night shift and, to make matters worse, I just drove for almost an hour in a blinding snowstorm because medical professionals do not have the option of staying home during bad weather. I vow that I will not live in this cold, snowy location one more winter. I'll move somewhere warm. Somewhere it never snows. Somewhere ice storms don't exist.

Miraculously that same week there's a classified ad in the local newspaper listing RN job openings at a new hospital in Florida. Sunny, warm, no snow, no ice Florida. I decide to inquire just out of curiosity.

It'll be hard to leave the area I've called home for most of my life but I really don't want to endure one more long, cold, dark winter in Massachusetts. Maybe this is just the ticket for me. It will be difficult to leave my family and friends but I'm young and what better time to pull up roots and start fresh in the Sunshine State?

I call the number and they offer to fly me down to interview for a position. I'm so excited but I don't discuss it with anyone because I'm simply on a fact-finding mission. Maybe they won't be interested in me. Maybe I won't like the location or facility. Maybe I'll get cold feet and not be adventuresome enough to leave my comfort zone and family.

It's certainly a life-changing decision, but what do I have to lose? I've never been to Florida so the free trip there for the interview will be a bonus in itself. Also, I'll be free of the winter weather for a couple of days. I agree to fly to Florida for the interview.

The warm sunshine bathes my face and washes away my winter woes. If I were at home I would be shoveling out my car before driving on the snowy roads to work. I would be pulling on my snow boots, parka, hat, gloves and scarf. I would be chilled to the bone as I walked from the parking lot to the hospital entrance. That is certainly nothing I would miss! Maybe this is going to work out for me.

The interview goes well and I'm impressed with the facility and the personnel. The thought of never having to deal with snow or ice again is almost impossible to fathom. Living someplace that experiences the change in seasons can be nice with the exception of winter and in Florida there is no winter. There may be some chilly nights or maybe even a flurry now and then but no winter weather like I've known since childhood. I've never been a snow worshipper so I wouldn't miss outdoor winter activities. I know the summers can be brutal with the heat, humidity and excessive bug population, but still no bitter cold or snow, ever.

After spending the night, I board an early flight back to Massachusetts. They say they'll be in contact with me after all the applicants have been interviewed and the final hiring decisions have been made. We circle the airport several times; the visibility is near zero due to the falling snow and wind. This would not happen in Florida.

I know that if I don't make the decision to move at this point in my life I probably never will. The longer I stay here, the harder it will be for me to leave. But do I really want to leave everything I know and move thousands of miles away from family and friends simply to escape the grips of winter? I have an extremely important and life-changing decision to make if I am offered the job.

Two days later I receive the call I'm waiting for: I've been selected for one of the open RN positions and they'd like me to report to work by the end of the month. I have less than a month to pack my belongings, leave my current job, find a new apartment in Florida and start on my new adventure in

the land of sunshine. No more cold, snow-filled win-
ter months for me. I am going to Florida!

The bus screeched to a stop to miss a deer running across
the road. Sara was thrown against the seat in front of her,
interrupting her relocation to Florida.

Sara would probably be in a retirement home in Florida
now had she moved there but then she never would have met
David or lived in the wonderful cottage by the sea, or spent
so much wonderful time with Michael. Her life would have
been totally different had she not decided at the twelfth hour
to stay in Massachusetts.

The driver walked through the bus to be sure that no one
was injured. Everyone was okay, just shaken a bit. One passenger in the rear of the vehicle threw out expletives that would
have made a sailor blush. Another called it a near-death experience.

This certainly was going to be a trip to remember; it would
provide forage for dinner conversation for days to come. Sara
glanced up to Joseph. He looked back her way. Their eyes met.
Did he wink? There must have been something in his eye.

Sara thought about these *what if* moments she'd been
experiencing. They presented themselves in great detail. Her
mind was taking her on journeys of possible lives different
from the one she had lived. Was she losing her mind slowly,
one life decision at a time? Why was this happening and how
long would it continue? Did she need medical attention?
Were these moments a precursor of future neurological trouble?

The residents slowly disembarked and headed for the
lobby. The cool September afternoon made Sara think one
more time about all the ways her life could have been different if she taken the position in Florida. But she didn't and she
lived in Massachusetts and had for almost all her life except

for the years she was in Ireland. Maybe that wasn't such a bad thing. She was no longer required to go out in the bad weather to go to work or anyplace else. She could stay warm inside waiting for the winter to melt into spring.

Once inside, everyone started to tell those who hadn't been on the outing about the incident on the bus ride back. It was front-page news. Sara saw Joseph out of the corner of her eye walking toward the elevator. Sara followed as inconspicuously as possible. She wanted to spend a couple of minutes alone with him. She felt a youthful flirtation stirring within. It was embarrassing but also a little exciting.

Unfortunately Jan, Betsy and Joseph all entered the elevator together with Sara jumping (okay, walking briskly) after them. Jan and Betsy had declined the mini golf outing. Joseph calmly explained, "The bus swerved and stopped suddenly on the way back to avoid a deer. Some of the people were a bit shaken up and one used words that I've heard in R-rated movies. No one was hurt. I think you'll hear all about it over supper. You ladies missed the excitement."

Jan smacked Betsy on the arm saying, "I told you we should have played miniature golf. We missed all the action. Next time I'm not going to let you talk me out of it. We need to get out more. I keep telling you, we need to get out more."

Sara and Joseph exited on the third floor. Jan continued to chatter away as the doors closed. Sara looked into Joseph's crystal blue eyes and asked, "Would you be interested in joining me for a cup of afternoon tea?"

Joseph smiled. "I would be delighted."

The view of the gardens from the veranda was perfect in the warm afternoon sun. This could be the start of a very special friendship! No way was she allowing Jean to get her claws into Joseph.

Nope, that was not going to happen.

Chapter Eight:
Involvement

relationships

Fall arrived with colorful foliage, cooler temperatures and most importantly, preparations for the annual Parliament Square Halloween Party. Had three months actually passed since she arrived here?

The dinner conversation for the past several weeks centered on what costumes the residents planned to wear, what games would be played at the celebration following the parade and the most exciting part: which friends and family to invite to the event. Sara was a bit hesitant to get involved as she was never a person who actively celebrated the traditional Halloween holiday. Never having children, she hadn't experienced the excitement of costumes and parades since she was a little girl.

She and David had attended several adult Halloween parties over the years. She remembered back to her favorite couple's costume. They were quite young then and both avid golfers; they exercised regularly and stayed trim and toned. Sara thought they would look great as Tarzan and Jane. She wasn't a seamstress, so making the costumes herself was out of the question. She rented them instead. David's initial reaction to his skimpy outfit was outward refusal, followed by fervent hesitation, culminating in compromising acceptance. He would wear the outfit if Sara found a manly chest shirt because he was not going to the party bare-chested. Sara found the shirt and they looked wonderful in their matching animal-print revealing outfits!

Sara invited Michael to attend the Halloween parade and party which was being held on the Saturday before the 31st. She hadn't heard back from him yet about whether he could attend. She was hopeful that he would, but if not she would celebrate with the rest of the residents and their guests. Sara's three closest friends, who lived near her cottage by the sea, no longer drove after dark and transportation was a problem for them. Maybe Michael would offer to bring them, too.

Sara sent them each an invitation but she hadn't received a reply. She had talked with them several times since moving to Parliament Square. They were all still lucky enough to be living in their own homes.

Diane and Carol were several years younger than Sara, but Michele, her college roommate, was the same age. Diane and Carol still lived with their husbands. Michele's husband passed away two years ago and she still hadn't come to terms with her loss. Sara could empathize with Michele; acceptance of David's death and the ability to move on had been a lengthy process for her.

This was the first Wednesday that Sara would be helping out at the daycare center. She was excited but also a bit nervous to meet the children. Youngsters can be brutally honest. It can be cute but it can also be a bit embarrassing.

Several veteran residents were there and they helped Sara acclimate to the daily routine. They warned her not to wear any garments that couldn't be laundered as there were plenty of spills and activities involving liquids or sticky substances. If assigned to the nursery, she could expect a plethora of possible blemishes and bodily fluid stains. This sounded better and better every minute. Maybe this wasn't the best fit for her. She changed her mind when she saw the cherub-like faces of the youngsters in the playroom. They came in all colors, shapes and sizes, some with full heads of curly locks, some with cute little pigtails, some with hardly any hair at all. She wanted to hug them all. One little towhead walked up to Sara and told her she looked just like her grammy. That made Sara feel incredibly special. This was going to work out just fine. Just fine indeed!

Sara had lunch in the dining room after she finished her volunteer time in the daycare center at noon. She was a bit weary from her active morning with the children but she experienced an inner contentment that she hadn't felt since coming to Parliament Square. At least on Wednesday and Friday mornings she had a reason to get out of bed. Now she had a purpose. There were still five other days of the week, but this was a start. Michael would be proud of her for taking the initiative to get involved.

Sara ordered the tuna salad on rye toast with lettuce and tomato. When she first moved in she disliked the food served in the dining room but as her attitude improved, so did the taste of the food. Was that a coincidence? Today she found it quite tasty even though she heard the usual complaints from the others. Sometimes she thought they said those things just to start a conversation.

There were a couple of menu items that Sara tended to stay away from but for the most part, and to her great surprise, the cuisine pleased her.

David always loved her cooking. He raved about her meals to friends sometimes to the point that Sara was a bit embarrassed. After she lost David she cut back on her cooking and many evenings she settled for a peanut butter sandwich or a bowl of cereal. Cooking for oneself was just not the same as cooking for others. Now she was actually glad that she no longer spent hours in the kitchen preparing meals.

After lunch Sara returned to her apartment and settled down with a good book and Penelope on her lap. She would check her mailbox before dinner to see if anyone had responded to the Halloween invitations.

She gave a lot of thought to what she might wear to the parade. Since sewing her own costume was not an option, she would either have to purchase one or make a costume that didn't require sewing. She thought about cutting a hole in a laundry basket, filling it with laundry and going as a full basket of laundry. Sara saw that on a television program and thought it was a cute idea. Maybe a cut-out Clorox bottle for a hat?

She always wanted to be a Disney princess when she was younger but probably the window of opportunity for her to do that had closed. She would definitely sign up for the Halloween store outing on Friday to explore her options. She was sure of one thing: She would positively not go as Jane this year or any other year from now on.

Sara's book held her interest for a while but the morning in the daycare center had tired her out and she felt herself drift off into another time and place. She was a young nurse working in a Boston hospital...

Here I am stuck working yet another weekend shift. The newer RNs seem to always be at the top of the list for weekend assignments. Seniority makes a difference in the work schedule. Although I have no exciting plans for most weekends I don't like having nearly every weekend taken from me.

Kevin, a third-year medical resident in cardiac surgery, asks me to go skiing with him over the weekend. We met in the operating room several months ago and our relationship kindled. We're not exclusive or seriously involved but I hope that might change.

Living in Massachusetts I certainly have access to plenty of snow and ski resorts. After several lessons I'm surprised to discover that I like skiing and I'm really not half bad at it.

On my weekends off I spend time on the slopes whenever possible. Kevin has skied since he was a child. My parents had been too busy with their careers when I was growing up to take us on skiing trips. I'm glad that I decided to try the sport even though I never thought of myself as a winter person.

As the ski season draws to a close for another year, Kevin and I are able to schedule a weekend trip. I'm quite excited as this is our first weekend trip together. I've been in other relationships since losing Andrew but none were very serious. I feel a connection with Kevin and I think he feels the same way about me.

We have a great weekend with perfect weather. We share intimacy for the first time in our relationship and it is phenomenal. The weekend is the best time I've had in years. I wake with a smile on my face, a bounce in my step and a new outlook on life. It's been a long time coming.

We join Kevin's parents for dinner and they are delightful. Although Kevin can't meet my father in Ireland, we do visit my mother and stepfather for the Memorial Day weekend. Being physicians, Kevin and my mother have much in common and the trip is a success. We talk about our future together.

Then the unexpected happens. Kevin's high school sweetheart, who met and married someone while Kevin was at medical school, tells him her husband is having an affair and she wants a divorce. She needs someone to talk to and that someone is Kevin.

He doesn't hide any of this from me and I encourage him to meet with her. I imagine that he'll discuss the next steps for her in her marriage and tell her about his relationship with me. Although she plays on Kevin's kind nature, he tells her that he plans to build a life with me and that she needs to move on to the next stage in her own life.

Kevin and I have a wonderful and full life together. Although we decide not to adopt children, we share so many interests that our years are both fulfilling and happy. We grow old together and move to a retirement village that encourages couples to remain active as long as physically possible. We share one another's lives well into our nineties.

A clap of thunder and Penelope's startled jump were enough to awaken Sara. She tried to review her *what if* moment, but she couldn't stop herself from thinking about what really happened.

When she encouraged Kevin to meet with his high school sweetheart the result was not what she expected. Kevin realized that he still loved her and, although he and Sara enjoyed something special together, it didn't have the depth of what he felt for his first true love. Kevin and Sara amicably (more so for him than for her) ended their relationship and Kevin married his first true love the following year.

Sara's heart was broken but little did she know that if Kevin's high school sweetheart hadn't returned she might never have met the true love of *her* life, the man who became her second husband, David. She'd never thought about that before.

She did love Kevin but not in the same way she loved Andrew and David. She realized as she grew older that there are many levels of love. Some love was sheer physical attraction, while other love was a total connection, a you-are-my-everything kind of love. Some love was convenience. Some love was desperation. Some love was even defiance.

Sara and David's love grew stronger and more committed with each passing year. That was not to say that there weren't bumps in the road along the way. No marriage was perfect but theirs was better than most. They could finish each other's sentences. They knew what the other was going to say before the words were spoken. They were two people combined into one. It was beautiful! But it was over too soon. They should have held hands and walked into the evermore together.

Although people grieve for the spouse who dies, we really ought to grieve for the survivor. They have to continue on life's journey alone without their soulmate. The time they spent together from morning until night for decades can no longer be shared. There's no one to share morning coffee with or complain about the weather with or laugh at a funny TV show with or share an evening meal and watch the news with. Instead there is emptiness, loneliness and silence.

Sara tried to derail this depressing train of thought. She had come to grips with losing David, as challenging as that process had been. She realized one morning several years ago that she had grieved long enough and now she needed to move on with her life. As difficult as it was for her to do, it was her only choice. David would understand. David would want her to go on without him.

She knew exactly what Joseph was going through right now. He needed time to grieve before he could move on with his life. The grieving process is different for each of us. Some need more time than others, and for some the process is never really finished. For the unfortunate widows or widowers who are unable to find closure, life will never again be happy and complete.

The thunderstorm that moved through while Sara rested filled the air with the clean scent of rain. She opened the doors to the veranda and stepped outside. There was a definite chill in the air. Fall was here and soon winter would follow.

The seasons, like life, change whether we want them to or not. The aging process can be difficult, laden with health issues and the loss of independence and loved ones, but as much as we try it cannot be stopped without ending life itself. The sooner we realize that, the better.

Sara freshened up and decided that she would go to the lobby and socialize a bit before dinner. She felt that she needed more companionship than Penelope could provide. She needed some adult conversation.

The lobby was rather quiet. She remembered the beauty-parlor coupon she won at her first bingo night. Maybe she should get her hair dyed pink and purple like the younger women were doing. Wouldn't that be something to talk about at dinner? No, that might be a bit much.

A simple color, cut and style would be good. Although many of the women allowed their hair to be gray, white or some combination of both, Sara vowed she would always keep her hair the auburn color of her youth. She would not let age rob her of the ability to keep her hair the color she wanted it to be.

The beauty shop was closed for the day, but there was always tomorrow. It would be nice to be pampered a bit. Maybe she would get a manicure too, or better yet a mani/pedi as the young people called it these days.

When Sara got to the dining room both of the seats next to Joseph were already taken. She took an empty chair between Jim and Jan. The conversation focused on what costumes to wear for the upcoming Halloween event. Mary said she was not going to attend. No big surprise there. Jan and Betsy were going as the Dynamic Duo, not much of a surprise since they appeared to be hinged at the hip. Betsy said, "I am going to be Batman and Jan will be Robin. We flipped a coin to decide that since we both wanted to dress as the Dark Knight. It worked out for the best because Jan has nicer legs than I do to wear the Robin tights."

Jan's necklace du jour was turquoise, huge, and color coordinated with her floor-length caftan. Betsy marveled at the colors of the evening sky after the storm. "Look at the sky. It's just so beautiful. I'm going to take a picture of it before our food comes." Sara wondered how many pictures were on Betsy's smartphone. She was always taking pictures. Sara often wished she could get excited over such little things.

Jim told one of his countless humorous stories as dinner was being served. "They say don't make old people really mad. A life sentence to them isn't that much of a threat!" That was funny and sad at the same time. The older Sara got the more she realized that the number of years she already lived were far greater than the number of years that remained. This was reality and reality was hard to accept.

Chapter Nine:
Participation

true love

After dinner, Joseph mentioned that he needed to check his mailbox and Sara said she'd walk along with him because she needed to check hers too. Joseph said that he really didn't feel like taking part in the Halloween activities, but Linda had twisted his arm into sending an invitation to his daughter, Allison. Joseph knew she was busy with her husband and two sons and he didn't want to infringe on her time.

Joseph mentioned how, when he raised his family, there never seemed to be enough hours in the day to get everything done. Allison was currently in that phase of her life's journey: working, raising her family, maintaining her home.

In youth, days are short and years are long. In old age, years are short and days are long. The years and decades pass quickly while life keeps us too busy to notice. One day you wake up to discover the person you were while building a career, raising a family and being physically and mentally active has been replaced with someone else. While Sara's mortality had always been a given, death always seemed impossibly far away. Now it taunted her when she looked in the mirror. Seriously, who was that old person staring back at her?

In her mailbox was a reply from Michael: He was coming to the Halloween event and he'd be happy to bring any of her friends along, But he wasn't wearing a costume. Sara hoped he'd change his mind about the costume and surprise her. She hadn't heard from Carol, Diane or Michele yet, but it was good to know that Michael would provide transportation for them. She hopes *they'll* wear costumes if they can make it. Joseph didn't get any mail. Maybe tomorrow. "Sara, do you play pinochle?" he asked.

"Yes, I do," she said. "David and I used to play with friends all the time."

Joseph raised his eyebrows. "Want to play cards?"

The activity room was nearly empty (such a change from the noise and crowds of bingo night). Celeste and Jean were there trying to recruit two more pinochle players. What a coincidence. They find an open table, two decks of pinochle cards (double deck is the only way to play) and seat themselves.

Joseph dealt the first hand and the bidding began. Jean doted on everything Joseph said and did. Sara remembered Jean's comment on the bus the day of the miniature golf outing: *I'm going to reel him in and make him mine.* She didn't think that Jean would be a good match for Joseph. Sara was going to keep an eye on her.

Sara had no claims to Joseph but she felt that he reciprocated her interest. He was Sara's pinochle partner. He sat at her dining room table each day. He has spent time alone with her discussing personal issues. She definitely held a lot of cards, so to speak.

For a moment she felt like a young school girl vying for the attention of a male classmate, or at least she thought she remembered what that felt like years and years and years ago.

Pinochle was fun and Sara remembered the game's subtleties as the evening progressed, even though focusing on the cards bothered her eyes a little. Her vision had deteriorated a bit due to AMD but her ophthalmologist had told her about new treatments using embryonic stem cell therapy. She was hopeful their research would provide some healing in the near future to halt and possibly reverse her vision loss.

Sara and Joseph reached the five-hundred-point mark first and were declared the winners. She hadn't played pinochle since losing David. She no longer had her pinochle partner or her life partner and, until today, she didn't want to play with any other partner. She and David had spent many evenings playing with friends. They had taken bridge lessons when they were younger, but they thought the game was for old people. Maybe now was the time to learn bridge.

The card game helped the evening pass quickly. Shortly after the game concluded Sara began to feel weary. Even though Jean was deep in conversation with Joseph, Sara said her goodbyes and headed for her room. Celeste followed her. "Sara, when do you plan to join the bingo evening again? It's really a lot of fun and they have better prizes now."

"I plan to attend in the coming weeks. Maybe I can have Joseph join us next time," she answered.

Sara shared her recent decision to spend time in the day-care center two mornings a week. They also chatted about going to the Halloween store the next day. Celeste loved the parade and confessed that she planned to purchase a terribly scary costume this year. As Sara exited the elevator she turned to Celeste. "I'll see you tomorrow for the trip to the Halloween store. I'm looking forward to it. I hope I'll find a costume that will make me look ten years younger and twenty pounds thinner. Wouldn't that be great?"

Sara spent a little time with Penelope on her lap before preparing for bed. Today had been the busiest day since coming to Parliament Square and she welcomed the fatigue. It was good to feel tired both physically and mentally for a change.

She switched on the television to catch the nightly news and weather, something she infrequently did because of all the bad news being broadcast every day. In this day and age news traveled fast, almost too fast. She remembered her parents watching the evening news to listen to both good and bad reports presented on a daily basis.

Today it seemed to Sara that the bulk of the news programs focused on local, national and international bad news. In fact, the viewer could watch upsetting, argumentative and depressing news broadcasts any time of the day or night. It never stopped being available to those who chose to watch.

Sara was not one of those people. These programs were not to her liking.

When Sara awoke on Friday morning her first thought was that she had to be at the daycare center at nine. She had a reason to get out of bed today. She would have to hurry a bit to get ready, eat breakfast in the dining room and walk the short distance to the daycare center. She was thankful that Michael had encouraged her to get involved and she patted herself on the back for taking his advice.

As she chose her apparel for the day she remembered the advice she was given about wearing comfortable, easily laundered clothes. She selected a pair of navy capris, a long-sleeved navy print blouse with a cream colored cotton sweater. The walk to the daycare center was short and the cooler, crisp fall weather didn't yet require a coat. Soon, wearing warm clothing would be necessary. Not Sara's favorite time of the year, especially in the Northeast.

Sara bade Penelope farewell and headed for the dining room, enticed by the aroma of freshly brewed coffee. Maybe today she would choose regular over decaf. She would need the caffeine to keep up with the youngsters. Joseph and Mary were absent but the others were seated and waiting for breakfast. Fresh blueberries on the pancakes this morning were a welcome sight.

Jim supplied the table with his normal dose of levity. "I saw a woman the other day who looked really, really old which wasn't out of the ordinary until she mentioned that she remembered going to high school with me." Pam found that especially funny and burst into laughter spraying a mouthful of partially chewed pancakes into the air. She apologized profusely while attempting to clean the blue mess off the tablecloth. That was definitely going to leave a stain.

While the others were finishing their breakfast, Joseph approached the table. He looked a bit tired and there was no sparkle in his blue eyes. "I was up later than normal last night and I'm having trouble getting awake this morning. That Jean sure can talk a guy's ear off. Maybe I could get some coffee intravenously."

Sara excused herself from the table, telling Betsy and Jan that she was on her way to the daycare center while trying to ignore Joseph's remark about Jean. The breakfast conversation continued as she walked away.

There was a bite in the air as the chilly fall breeze hit Sara's face upon exiting the building. It was only a short distance and although transportation was available, she chose to walk while she was still able. Sometimes walking helped ease the arthritic pain in her knees.

She absorbed the beauty of the colorful foliage around Parliament Square. The colors were brilliant this year. Some years the leaves were more vivid than others and this was one of those years. Many people traveled to New England to experience the breathtaking fall foliage. Sara didn't have to travel to partake of nature's fall parade of colors.

Upon entering the daycare center Sara felt a twinge of excitement, or maybe anticipation, about the morning's activities. The children were playing games, coloring, block building and just generally being kids. One of the facilitators asked Sara if she would like to read a story to the children today. They had story time each morning at ten for the three and four-year-old children. Sara replied that she would enjoy doing that.

At ten the children were seated on the floor around the adult chair where Sara sat. Today's story was about a kitty who wandered away from his home and got lost. There were numerous pictures in the book and Sara stopped to show the children all of them as she read. The kitty climbed a tall, tall tree and the firemen had to rescue the kitty. The kitty was gently carried down the ladder and returned to his family safe and sound. The children were so happy that the kitty was rescued and reunited with his family.

Sara asked if anyone had kitties at their houses and that started a flurry of responses from the children. They were spontaneously verbal and more than willing to share with the group. The first book reading had gone well and Sara felt happy and purposeful today. It was a good feeling and hopefully the start of an upward trend to acceptance of her new residence and lifestyle. It certainly wasn't an overnight process but maybe, just maybe she could see a light at the end of the tunnel without hearing the sound of an approaching train.

The three hours passed quickly and Sara returned to the main building for lunch and hopefully an afternoon siesta with Penelope. The dining room was filling up as Sara seated herself at the table. Her dining companions were discussing the afternoon trip to the Halloween store in search of the perfect costumes. The bus would be departing promptly at three o'clock.

Sara had signed up for the trip several days ago. She quickly ate her lunch, exited the dining room and headed for her room in search of a bit of rest before the outing. Penelope met her at the door and rubbed against her legs to welcome her back. Having Penelope certainly boosted her spirits and provided much needed company and companionship.

She closed her eyes and almost immediately drifted into a dream about her beloved David. When asked how they met, she would always delight in telling people the story. She would say they met by accident which was exactly how they met.

Sara had finished working the overnight shift at the hospital. It was a gloomy fall morning with thick fog. The nurses coming in for the morning shift warned those leaving to be careful as visibility was close to zero. After logging her last patient report, she gathered up her belongings and headed for the parking lot.

The staff had reserved parking under the building and in the multi-tiered hospital parking garage. Sara had parked at roof level when she reported to work as the basement and other reserved parking levels were full. They really needed to add more reserved parking.

As she started to back out of her parking space another car, going too fast for conditions, passed behind her and clipped her fender. She was extremely unhappy; she pulled back into her parking space and got out to examine the damages. The driver of the other car apologized profusely and explained that he was late for an early morning presentation. He offered to cover any expenses to repair the damage. They exchanged insurance and contact information and were on their way.

Sara drove home, put the information on the kitchen counter, cooked breakfast and soon fell sound asleep. The phone woke her around three o'clock. She answered and heard the voice at the other end say his name was David Jennings and he wanted to apologize again for the accident that morning and to ensure that she wasn't injured.

He told her that he had reported the accident to his insurance company and they were going to contact her to schedule an appointment to assess the damage. She groggily thanked him for calling and closed her eyes to return to sleep. When she awoke later that afternoon she wasn't sure if someone named David had actually called or if she had dreamt the whole thing.

That evening, when she reported to work for the overnight shift, there was a message waiting for her. Someone had called that afternoon and left a number where he could be reached. The name of the caller was David Jennings. Sara put the note in her pocketbook and forgot about it until she searched her purse for her car keys the following morning. It was early so she decided to wait and return his call later that morning before going to bed.

She was a bit curious about what he needed to talk with her about that was so important so she decided to call him around ten o'clock. He answered on the third ring. She told David that she was returning his call and wondered if there was a problem with the insurance. She could not believe his answer. He called to confess to her that he had admired her from afar in the hospital cafeteria, which he frequently visited as a pharmaceutical representative, for some time. When he realized she was driving the car he hit, he regretted the accident but was happy to meet her in person.

He never had the nerve to approach her and had it not been for the accident, maybe he never would have. There was much more to discuss and he wondered if they could meet. Sara said that she was currently dating someone but maybe they should meet to discuss the estimate for the damages to her car and the insurance payment process.

They met for coffee in the hospital cafeteria the next day and the rest was history. They were kindred spirits and their love was spontaneous. Sara broke off her other relationship immediately.

From that moment on Sara would advise anyone in a relationship that, when and if you ever are fortunate enough to meet your perfect match, the one-in-a-million for you, don't hesitate for a minute. Jump in with both feet. She and David were married on New Year's Eve 1964 and lived happily ever after until she lost him in 2012.

The wonderful dream and memories of meeting, marrying and being spouses and friends for life with David was interrupted when Sara closed her eyes...

I am so tired. I'm going directly home this morning. The overnight shift always seems to last longer than the other shifts and it's riddled with issues and

*emergencies. The fog is dense and as I back out of
the parking spot a car races behind me.*

*I slam on the brakes and the car just misses hit-
ting me. I yell some expletives which no one hears
but me. I cautiously back out of the parking space
and head home so pleased that I have avoided that
jerk running into my car. I would report him but the
fog kept me from seeing his license plate. Maybe this
is going to be my lucky day!*

Sara's alarm clock brought her out of her dream. She
shook her head and tried to clear her thoughts. Was it possible that destiny made the accident happen, causing her to
meet her true love, soulmate and life's partner? Would she
have met David even if the accident hadn't happened? In the
grand scheme of life were some choices invisible forks in the
road? Decisions made devoid of input from us? Conclusions
formulated without us being part of the equation?

That was really something to think about. However, it
was something to think about later because now she had to
hurry to be on time for the Halloween store outing.

Chapter Ten:
Celebration

spooky

The short ride to the Halloween store was uneventful; no deer crossings, no screeching brakes. Sara sat with Celeste. She counted twenty-two passengers only five of whom she knew. Celeste, who had lived at Parliament Square for over five years, knew the names of almost everyone.

Celeste, it turned out, was a bit of a close talker, a term Sara remembered from a long ago *Seinfeld* episode. A close talker was a person who put their face very close to another's while talking. It made Sara uncomfortable. She never knew when she might be showered with saliva.

Celeste seemed nice enough but in addition to leaning in too close she was also loud enough for everyone else on the bus to hear what she was saying. She obviously needed a hearing aid. Every sentence Sara spoke she had to repeat, sometimes more than once.

The residents disembarked and were instructed to meet back at the bus at exactly four thirty. They had to be back at Parliament Square in time for the evening meal, which was served promptly at five. If anyone finished shopping before the designated departure time they were welcome to board the bus and wait for the others. They weren't to go anywhere but the Halloween store, and two of the aides from Parliament Square, Cindy and Brad, were available for assistance with shopping.

Sara remembered hearing these same instructions when she visited the zoo as a child with a group of youngsters. There were so many similarities between the very young and the elderly. Although she knew it was for her own safety, it felt unnecessary and demeaning.

The store was quite large and filled with everything Halloween. There were animated ghouls with scary sounds and flashing lights, grisly horror scenes, and oodles of costumes divided into sections based on age and gender.

Sara and Celeste walked to the adult women's aisle to peruse the possibilities. There were numerous costumes designed for younger, more voluptuous female figures. Those were definitely out of the question. She chuckled when she saw a Jane, of *Tarzan and Jane* fame, costume. Had she really been able to wear something that skimpy out in public? If she wore that to the parade this year she might scare the children more than she would if she dressed as a giant spider. Sara was disappointed to discover that the princess costumes didn't come in her size. That ship had apparently sailed.

There were political figure masks which could be worn with street clothes, superhero costumes complete with capes and matching masks, and the standard clown, gypsy, lion, cat, dog, etc. costumes. Sara wanted to find something unique and was still considering the laundry basket costume when the Little Red Riding Hood outfit caught her eye. It wasn't revealing, it wasn't form-fitting and best of all, it was on sale. She looked for one in her size, found it, and decided it would be her costume this year.

As she got ready to head to the register, Celeste jumped out of nowhere dressed as a Christmas tree with decorative lights and a hat topped with a blinking star the size of her head. "Gadzooks, woman! You scared the daylights out of me. You could give a woman my age a medical emergency doing that. Celeste, you will really "spruce up" the Halloween parade. That is a "tree-mendous" costume. Please don't surprise anyone else like that. They could have a heart attack."

Sara browsed around a bit more while her heart rate returned to normal. There was still some time until she had to pay and return to the bus. She literally bumped into Joseph because she was watching one of the talking displays and not paying attention. "Joseph, look at the costume I found. I think it's perfect. Have you found anything yet? They have a wonderful selection."

"Sara," Joseph said, "I'm not really interested in going but I'm trying to make an effort since my daughter called last evening to say she'd be here with my grandsons. This all seems a bit childish for a man my age. I've never been a big fan of Halloween."

"I understand," Sara replied. "Let me help you look. Maybe we can find something together."

Joseph reluctantly agreed. "I definitely do not want anything related to a politician. That's much too controversial in this day and age. Also, no superhero costume because who wants to see a man my age in tights and a cape? This all seems so silly."

They stumbled across the Big Bad Wolf costume from Little Red Riding Hood, exchanged glances and burst out laughing. Wouldn't it be a hoot (as the young folks say) for them to go as Little Red Riding Hood and the Big Bad Wolf? Joseph tried on the wolf mask which slipped entirely over his head, asked Sara how he looked and made a deep growling sound. They both laughed out loud and noticed other shoppers looking their way. Both headed for the cashier with their selections.

On the ride home Sara and Joseph shared a seat. Celeste looked a little unhappy when she saw them together but she recovered quickly when Brad asked her to sit with him. "Sara, thanks for helping me find a costume and boosting my spirits. You seem to be one of very few people capable of doing that at this point in my life. I really enjoy spending time with you. You are truly a caring person." Sara felt her cheeks flush and knew that she must be blushing but Joseph made no comment about it. She felt warm all over.

Halloween was on a Tuesday and the parade and party were being held on the Saturday prior to Halloween, the 28th. That was a week from tomorrow. Sara was anxious to go up to her room after dinner to try on the costume. She didn't want to admit it, but she was excited about the parade and party. It was something to look forward to, which was a good thing. Now she had the daycare center two mornings a week and the Halloween party to drive her life at a more purposeful level. And then there was time spent with Joseph.

The bus arrived at Parliament Square at exactly four fifty-five. The smell of spaghetti sauce filled the air and Sara's mouth watered. The activity of the trip made her very hungry. She hadn't expected that. Her appetite was often minimal at best.

Sara and Joseph joined the others at the table who were passing around a basket of warm garlic bread. Jan asked, "Sara, did you find a costume for the parade?"

"I'm keeping it a secret. You'll just have to wait."

Betsy spoke up. "Jan and I are going as Salt and Pepper shakers. My daughter is extraordinarily artsy and is making the costumes for us." A perfect choice, Sara thought, although she was disappointed that she wouldn't get to see the Batman and Robin costumes Jan mentioned earlier in the month.

Jim chimed in. "I'm coming as a clown. I hope I don't fall down wearing those oversized shoes. I may even try to juggle apples." A clown was a perfect choice for him, the resident comedian at their table.

Mary wouldn't be attending as she was spending that weekend away from Parliament Square with family. Deborah was undecided about it and Pam loudly announced "I'M COMING AS RAGGEDY ANNE. I ALREADY HAVE MY COSTUME." The hot dishes of spaghetti were served and the dinner conversation quieted.

Sara hurried to her apartment after she finished eating. She was anxious to try on her costume and Penelope needed to be fed her dinner. It had been a long day and Sara was genuinely tired for a change, not just from sheer boredom and lack of purpose. It was a good feeling and she looked forward to a long restful sleep.

She looked at herself in the full-length mirror after she donned the Little Red Riding Hood outfit. Instead of the paunchy old lady in her wrinkled birthday suit she saw a determined woman of age dressed as a character out of a Grimm Brothers fairy tale. Seems like just yesterday she was reading the story to young Michael; never in her wildest dreams imagining she'd one day be dressed as the leading character.

She was pleased that she selected this costume. It was colorful without being gaudy. It was age appropriate in style and proportion. Even better, it showed off her still attractive legs which had always been one of her better attributes. The best feature of all was that her costume directly connected her to Joseph as the Big Bad Wolf. They might be seen as a couple and that was okay with Sara. She was getting to like Joseph more as their paths crossed over the passing weeks.

After a good night's sleep Sara awakened refreshed and— dare she say it?— a bit spry. Her attitude was much improved and she was beginning to accept Parliament Square as her permanent residence. However, if offered the ability to move back to her cottage by the sea, she would pack her bags immediately.

She had come to terms over the past several weeks with the reality of the situation. Age had robbed her of the ability to safely live alone in her home. Michael had recognized the signs for some time before moving her to Parliament Square, but he allowed his Aunt Sara to stay in her cottage as long as possible. She reminded herself once again that she was lucky to have Michael in her life.

People of advanced age and declining health often have no one to assist them. They remain in their home living alone, sometimes an extremely isolated and unhappy existence. It's sad to think the average lifespan is constantly increasing while the physical health, mental capability and ability to live independently often don't support those additional years. Places like Parliament Square should be applauded for providing seniors a caring, safe and activity-driven environment to fill their twilight years.

After a brief bit of soul searching and Penelope time, Sara showered, dressed and headed to the dining room for breakfast. This was going to be a good day. Hopefully it was the first of many to come. Some of her dining companions were absent; it was Saturday which was sometimes a day for visits from family and friends or a day trip like the one she had enjoyed with Michael.

Next Saturday was the much anticipated Halloween parade and party. Today she would check her mailbox to see if she received any responses from the three friends she invited. The breakfast conversation centered on changes in medications, recent doctor visits and sleep patterns.

Conversation changes radically over the years. We focus on relationships, fashion choices, weddings and babies when we're young adults, switch to careers, children and life goals when we're middle aged, progress to grandchildren, retirement and downsizing options later in life, and conclude with health, medical procedures, medications, and funerals during our twilight years. Like it or not, such is the circle of life.

The mail was still being sorted when Sara arrived to check her box. She saw an envelope in her bin, plucked it out and took it with her to one of the floral sofas in the lobby area. The return address indicated it was from her friend Michele who had been Sara's college roommate many decades ago. She opened the letter hoping to see a positive response about attending the Halloween event. Instead she saw something much, much better.

Michele was moving to Parliament Square! Sara was going to have a friend living here. She would have someone from

ELAINE C. BAUMBACH

her past to share her future with, just like Jan and Betsy. This
was the best news she could receive. She was so excited. She
couldn't wait to share the news with Michael and the others.

The week before the parade and party literally flew by.
Sara was busy with the childcare center Wednesday and Friday mornings. She chatted with Michele on the phone and
they shared some wonderful conversations. It would probably
be November or December until Michele would arrive and
Sara couldn't wait.

Sara hadn't seen Joseph much this week. Their paths
crossed in the dining room but no more pinochle games or
talks on the veranda. She thought he seemed to be coping
with the loss of his wife a bit better some days when she saw
him having animated conversations with Jim at dinner. She
still felt an attraction to him but maybe it wasn't reciprocated.
They were friends and that was good enough for now.

The day of the Halloween parade and party arrived. It was
a brisk October day. Due to the high winds the parade was
going to be held indoors this year. Sara expected Michael to
arrive shortly before 3:30 when the festivities were scheduled
to begin. Unfortunately, none of Sara's friends were able to
attend, but next year Michele would be there as both a friend
and a neighbor.

The residents were instructed to gather in the lobby at
3:25. The long wait was over. It was show time! Sara checked
her costume in the full-length mirror. She felt that she did jus-
tice to the Little Red Riding Hood character. She was anxious
to see how Joseph looked in his Big Bad Wolf costume. Maybe
they could walk together in the parade?

She looked forward to spending some time with Michael
after the parade. Since the Saturday they had spent together
several weeks ago, she had talked with him on the phone but
missed seeing him. He used to visit her at her cottage to share
dinner or to take long walks on the beach. His job kept him

incredibly busy and the drive to Parliament Square took about thirty minutes compared to a less than five-minute drive to her cottage. She understood why he visited less frequently, but that didn't stop her from missing him.

There was a flurry of activity when the elevator doors opened at the lobby. Residents were bedecked in their costumes waiting for the parade to begin. Sara spotted Michael on the sofa closest to the entrance. She waved to him; he smiled and waved back. He hadn't dressed for the parade which disappointed her a little, but he had warned her that he was not going to wear a costume. She wondered if he felt her costume was silly and inappropriate for her age.

Before she could give it any more thought Linda announced, via her battery-powered megaphone, that everyone was to form a line starting at the back of the activity room. Sara looked for the Big Bad Wolf but hadn't spotted him yet. As she made her way to the activity room she saw someone else dressed as Little Red Riding Hood. When she got closer she could see that it was Jean. She was trying to get the Big Bad Wolf's attention. She wanted to give Jean a special one finger wave but restrained herself. That wouldn't be ladylike or appropriate in front of the others in attendance.

Jean grabbed Joseph by the arm and Sara overheard her tell him they should march together. That was something Sara did not see coming.

The parade began as "The Monster Mash" blasted from huge speakers; the festive event was underway. Sara could see people taking pictures, little children laughing and cheering for family members, and Michael looking especially pleased as Sara marched through the lobby. She was having a wonderful time in spite of the fact that Jean had commandeered the Big Bad Wolf to walk with her in the parade.

Maybe Joseph was happy for the change of plans, or maybe he never intended to pair up with Sara during the parade. It really didn't matter. She enjoyed the music, the parade and the visit from Michael. Betsy and Jan looked great as large salt and pepper shakers. Pam made a perfect Raggedy Ann. *Focus on the good*, she thought, as senior citizens must accept every new day as a present. She smiled her best, biggest smile and enjoyed the rest of the parade.

The dining room was decorated with pumpkins—some carved, some artfully painted—ears of Indian corn, bales of straw and baskets of apples. There was hot apple cider, freshly made donuts and a popcorn machine with buttered popcorn. Sara spotted Michael and they sat together at a table enjoying the refreshments. Joseph was talking with his daughter and grandsons at a table across the room.

There were many family members and friends. It was nice to see the residents enjoying themselves instead of worrying about some age-related concern, ache or pain. It was a time to put problems and worries on the back burner. Sara thought the younger generation's phrase "living in the moment" was a perfect slogan for the day.

For a moment Sara thought she was going to experience another lapse into a what-might-have-happened scenario, but it didn't materialize. Maybe those episodes were over now that she was more comfortable with her surroundings. Maybe they were orchestrated by her brain in an effort to relieve some of her anxiety and unhappiness. Maybe she should seek medical attention. No, she didn't want more tests, more doctor appointments, possibly more medications. She was fine. Her mind just showed her what could have been. She wasn't hearing voices or seeing little green men in space ships.

As the festivities wound down and Sara walked Michael to the lobby, Joseph and his daughter stopped them. They introduced each other. Allison thanked Sara for helping her father during this difficult time in his life. "Would it be possible for me to call you sometime soon to chat a bit? I'm so grateful that you and Dad are able to share time together."

Sara replied, "That's fine with me. I would enjoy that."

As Joseph walked Allison through the lobby, Sara turned to Michael. "I received a note from my college friend, Michele, and she's going to be moving to Parliament Square. Can you believe it? I'm going to have a friend living right here with me. Isn't that wonderful news? We've been friends for decades. I've been starting some new friendships since moving here, especially Joseph, but this will be someone with whom I have history. This is someone who knew me when I was young. Someone I can laugh with about memories of days gone by. Someone I can truly call my friend."

Michael was very glad to hear the news and thought to himself that Michele moving here might be just what his aunt needed. Maybe the pieces were going to fit together for his aunt after all. "That's wonderful, Aunt Sara. You'll have someone to share your time with. That is indeed good news!"

Chapter Eleven: Anticipation

parenting

ara hated to see the evening come to a close. Michael gave her a hug. "I'll call you next week to set up another Saturday outing in November. I can't tell you enough how proud I am of your volunteer work in the daycare center, your involvement in the Halloween event and, most of all, your new attitude about life here. You've come a long way and I couldn't be happier. I'm especially pleased to hear that Michele is coming to Parliament Square. You are in a safe environment making new friends and soon sharing your time with an old friend. I couldn't be more pleased for you."

When she returned to her apartment after saying goodbye, Sara removed her Little Red Riding Hood costume and carefully put it on a hanger. Maybe she could walk with the Big Bad Wolf next year. Or maybe she would choose a different costume. Next Halloween seemed a long time away and she often kidded with others that she stopped buying green bananas after her eightieth birthday. One day at a time, she told herself. *One day at a time.*

The autumn weeks passed quickly. The colorful leaves dropped from the trees and the colder winter temperatures arrived. Sara was excited about the next event, the annual Sadie Hawkins dance. Due to the fact that women far outnumbered men at Parliament Square, it was made perfectly clear that inviting a woman to the dance was acceptable.

Allison, Joseph's daughter, called a few days after the Halloween party. She told Sara that her father confided in her that Jean seemed to be a nice woman but he felt that she was trying to push herself on him and he didn't appreciate or reciprocate the interest.

He said that Sara was the only resident who shared quality time with him and for that he was appreciative, but he wasn't ready to make any commitments as he felt it would be disrespectful to his wife's memory. He was still broken hearted about losing his soulmate and it would take him time to adjust to his loss, if that was even possible. Female companionship was wonderful, he truly missed it, but starting over in his eighties would be challenging to say the least.

Sara was delighted to hear this. She wasn't ready to initiate a relationship either, but she loved spending time with a male friend. Female friends were wonderful and she so anticipated Michele's arrival at Parliament Square, but it wasn't the same as a friendship with someone of the opposite sex.

At her age it certainly wasn't a lustful attraction (although intimacy in her eighties was not out of the question) but rather a friendship with a male connection. It was hard to put the dissimilarity into words but there were distinct differences between male and female companionship.

Sara continued to volunteer at the daycare center. It was one of the best decisions she'd made since coming to Parliament Square. The mornings she spent there seemed to fly by and she felt that she was making a real contribution. The children for the most part were quite well behaved, very social and so darn cute. Sophie, a blonde four-year-old, took a liking to Sara and always greeted her with a big hug. It was heartwarming and she basked in the warmth of Sophie's little-girl affection.

After all this time her heart still ached for the daughter she lost. She and David mutually decided not to pursue an adoption but she had questioned that decision many times. She and David lived a full life until David's passing, but she always wondered if they made the right decision about adoption.

One evening after dinner Sara and Joseph had the opportunity to chat a bit in the empty lobby. Joseph said, "I must admit I'm acclimating somewhat to life here although it's not where I expected to be at this point in my life. I always thought my wife would outlive me. Statistically, that should have been the case. Her sudden passing left me in a situation

I hadn't planned for or thought about. I would have preferred walking hand-in-hand through the pearly gates with Theresa. My life is so empty without her and although I'm making a real effort to move on, it's difficult."

Sara could see tears welling in his eyes as he spoke. "After losing David holidays, family gatherings, every part of life was no longer the same. I still have photos and memories and I still do a lot of the same things we did as a couple, but reminiscing can be painful and depressing. Sometimes I think living without David is more painful than the physical pain he experienced before he passed. People try to help, and I appreciate it, but it's like putting a Band-Aid on a broken bone. It doesn't make it better." Sara paused for a moment. "Joseph, would you be my escort to the Sadie Hawkins dance?"

Joseph said, "I would be delighted to be your escort for the evening. I was secretly hoping that you'd invite me before Jean. If she invited me I don't know what I would say. Now I can tell her that I've already been invited." Sara didn't know if she was more excited because Joseph said yes or because Jean would be turned down. She told herself that wasn't nice but she didn't care. Others wandered into the lobby and their one-on-one time ended.

Linda strolled in to remind everyone that the weekly bingo game would start in fifteen minutes. Maybe Sara would join another time, but not tonight. She wanted to return to her apartment and savor the fact that she and Joseph would be a couple for the Sadie Hawkins event. She reminded herself it was only a friendship because she respected Joseph's privacy and his need to mourn the loss of Theresa. But maybe someday, yes maybe someday, it would grow to be more.

Sara watched a new sitcom and petted Penelope who loudly purred on her lap. She caught herself laughing out loud a couple of times. She remembered back to the days when there was one television in the house and no remote control.

The person watching had to get up and walk to the TV to change the channel or coerce another family member to do it. In addition to that, only a handful of programs were available to watch each day.

Today there was a television in almost every room, complicated remotes that controlled the television and literally hundreds of programs available for viewing twenty-four hours a day, seven days a week. *My how things have changed,* she thought. She wondered what it would be like fifty years from now, not that she would be around to see it. Technology, like life, marches on whether we want it to or not.

The "good old days" were so uncomplicated, more slowly paced, and family oriented. Today the many vehicles of social media allow virtually real-time access to individual, local, national and world events. We call it progress, but does it really make life better? Requiring technical support to operate a television remote with fifty buttons on it to change a station, or to use a smartphone to make a simple telephone call, seemed excessive. But now she was talking like an old fogey, someone long in the tooth or a vintage adult as the younger generation put it. She remembered when she was a member of that generation.

Sara rested her head on the back of the chair and drifted to an earlier time, when she and David were newlyweds...

Before we were married, David and I talked about adopting a child. He is disappointed that I can't bear children. He always thought that he'd like to be a father after marrying the girl of his dreams, but he isn't totally comfortable with adoption.

He's extremely busy with his pharmaceutical representative career and is frequently required to travel overnight or longer to visit doctors and medical facilities. Additionally, I often work long shifts, sometimes overnight, at the hospital. His traveling and my shift work will make it difficult to raise a child.

We need both incomes to save and be able to purchase a house. David and I decide to submit some applications to adoption agencies but we're not in a hurry to become parents since we're both working on advancing our careers.

As luck would have it, when we least expect it a situation presents itself for which we are totally unprepared. A single mother who is a member of our church is killed in a tragic traffic accident and she leaves behind a two-year-old daughter, Cynthia. She has no immediate family and the church asks if a member of the congregation would be interested in fostering Cynthia with a possible adoption at a later date after the family tree is thoroughly researched for relatives.

Many of the families in the church are middle-aged or older and have already raised their children or have children in high school. Taking on a two-year-old is a definite life-changer. After much soul searching and discovering that Cynthia will be placed in the hands of child-care services if no members from the church volunteer, we step forward and offer to take her into our lives.

She is a cute little girl with curly red hair and a disposition to match. We are definitely challenged by this major change in our lifestyle but also grateful to have the opportunity to bond with this adorable little girl. I cut back some of my shifts at the hospital and David declines a promotion, which could have progressed to a vice presidency at his company.

It's an exceedingly difficult decision. David has worked hard for years to advance to his current position. He sacrificed many weekends and vacation days, worked long hours and traveled extensively to make this promotion possible. He can certainly keep his current position, work fewer hours and refuse extended travel opportunities but that will limit his career. It's a sacrifice he is willing to make. He loves being a father to Cynthia.

I quickly transition and become Cynthia's primary caregiver. She misses her mother terribly and we overcompensate for her loss. There are no more weekend dinner dates for David and me. Nights out with girlfriends became a thing of the past.

Having a child changes our lives in so many ways. We worry that some distant relative will be found and take Cynthia from us. Although it would be wonderful for Cynthia to know her blood relatives, we will be devastated if we aren't able to raise Cynthia as our daughter. She is an unexpected gift sent to us for a reason. We need her as much, or maybe more, than she needs us.

I receive a call at work from child services. I literally pray out loud that it isn't news about locating a blood relative.

The woman informs me that the search for a family member has officially hit a dead end and we are able to legally adopt Cynthia if we so desire. I shout "YES" so loudly that the nurse standing next to me spills her hot coffee all over a desk full of paperwork.

I immediately call David to share the good news. He is ecstatic and tells me no job or career is more important than having Cynthia as our daughter. We will be wonderful parents.

Sara awoke to the sound of sirens. It took her a moment to realize that it was the fire alarms blasting. This was either a real fire or possibly just a drill to ensure the residents knew where the fire exits were and how to safely exit the building.

Sara grabbed her purse, put Penelope in her carrier and left her apartment, locking the door behind her. Fortunately one of the aides appeared in the hallway directing people to safety and offered to carry Penelope. The residents were in a motley assortment of attire. Since it was almost nine o'clock at night, many were in pajamas, bathrobes, slippers or other nightwear, sometimes leaving little to the imagination.

Some had sunken jawlines where their dentures normally were. Others had hair in styles not normally seen in public. Some had removed their makeup for the night and looked ghostly pale and a hundred years old.

Anyone who was physically able to descend the staircase was encouraged to do so. Using the elevator in case of fire was dangerous as the electricity could go out and the passengers would be stranded between floors. Fortunately, there was a large generator on site, so there was an alternate source of energy in case of emergency.

Several fire trucks were outside the lobby with a sea of red lights flashing. Firemen dressed in full gear were hustling into the building. Since it was quite cold on this November evening, the residents were sent to the activity room. Sara spotted Deborah who normally projected a picture of perfection. She was clad in a Disney printed robe and matching slippers with no traces of makeup, her hair flattened to her head using some turban-like accessory. The fortunate few who hadn't prepared for sleep, like Sara, were still in street clothes and grateful for the decision not to retire early that night.

Linda talked to the crowd that were gathered in the activity room. "This is not a fire drill. A resident placed a bag of microwave popcorn in his microwave and pushed the incorrect setting causing the bag to catch on fire in the microwave. Although there may be residual smoke and the smell of burnt popcorn, there is no danger and everyone can begin an orderly return to your rooms for the night. We are so sorry for the inconvenience." The crowd began to disperse, some complaining about the person who caused the issue, some upset that they missed a portion of a television program, some embarrassed by how they were dressed, and one who was sad because the popcorn was ruined.

Sara returned to her room. Brad brought Penelope a moment later and declined Sara's offer of a tip. "All in a day's work," he said. Penelope scurried out and ran for cover under the rocking chair, frightened by all the noise and activity.

Sara's mind returned to her thoughts about the adoption of Cynthia. She often wondered how her life with David would have been different if they had chosen to make Cynthia a part of it.

At the time they discussed their options at great length, but Sara was too afraid that if they fostered Cynthia and blood relatives were located, she wouldn't be able to release the little girl without forever regretting the decision to foster the child. It was one the most difficult decisions of her life and to this day she was never sure if she made the correct choice.

Sara drifted off to sleep that night with a smile on her face anticipating the arrival of her friend Michele and the upcoming Sadie Hawkins dance. Her window of negative thoughts and concerns closed a bit and her window of positive thoughts and expectations opened wider. Carly Simon's "Anticipation" played in her head. It used to be one of her favorites. The lyrics began with "We can never know about the days to come." That verse was true at any age, but especially in the winter of your life.

Sweet dreams, Sara.

Chapter Twelve:
Acceptance

college days

The Sadie Hawkins event was quickly approaching. Sara remembered attending dances in high school and college where she invited a male classmate to celebrate Sadie Hawkins day. In this day and age, girls don't wait for Sadie Hawkins day to reverse the century-old trend that males initiate social invitations. The practical basis of a real Sadie Hawkins Day was one of simply reversing the traditional gender roles.

Sara remembered doing a short report on this pseudo holiday while in high school. The celebration of Sadie Hawkins Day originated in Al Capp's hillbilly comic strip *Li'l Abner*. Sadie Hawkins was a homely girl and when she turned thirty-five years old her father invented the day to allow Sadie to choose a boy suitor. The original event was a foot race where Sadie pursued the town's most eligible bachelors. The bachelor Sadie caught would be her husband. That was certainly different than the celebration of today. Now it was lady's choice dance with no expectation of matrimony.

Sara had become friendlier with her dining room tablemates. One evening at dinner Mary, who was normally private and not much of a talker, said, "My eldest daughter was recently diagnosed with breast cancer and is undergoing chemotherapy. She lives in Florida and I haven't seen her in almost two years. I'm very concerned. I feel helpless living so far away and not being able to be with her."

The other residents tried to provide Mary with some comforting words and prayers. Mary responded, "I hope to visit her soon and spend time with her. We talk on the telephone and Skype or FaceTime but it just isn't the same as being together and sharing hugs. We expect illness and disease to invade our bodies when we get old, but we don't expect it to happen to our children. I would trade places with her in a heartbeat if I could."

Getting older not only increases the chances of having personal health issues of our own, it also increases the chances that our adult children will have similar health issues as they themselves age. In life's normal progression, the expectation is that the circle of life (birth, survival, and death) takes the oldest first; however, that isn't always the case.

Losing a child at any age has to be one of the hardest experiences for a parent to go through as Sara understood all too well. The loss of a middle-aged or older adult son or daughter leaves the aged parent, who may already be struggling with age-related health issues, sad, lonely and asking why. If life followed a normal sequence, the parents would always pass away before their children and grandchildren.

The aged parent asks, *How could this happen?* and, *Who can I depend on now for support, assistance and encouragement?* As if getting older isn't bad enough, now the aging parent must do it alone without their son or daughter. Those who lose an only son or daughter are destined to live out their days without that child and possibly spiral into deep depression and despair. Losing a parent is expected but painful, losing a sibling is difficult, but losing a child is catastrophic. Sara pushed the crippling thoughts away and prayed especially hard for Mary's daughter.

Jim was always willing to share an opinion at the dinner table on the current state of political affairs or to dole out a bit of humor. His comic performances often started out as possible true stories until he arrived at the punch line. Sometimes there was laughter, sometimes there was a barrage of partially chewed food, sometimes there was loud groaning and occasionally total silence.

Today's story involved a geriatric gentleman who told his friend he was getting a tattoo like the younger generation was doing. The friend asked whether he chose a heart, a naked lady, a skull-and-crossbones or maybe a skeleton. The gentleman replied no, none of them; he was getting his name and address tattooed on his arm because he wasn't getting any younger. The punch line was funny but, sadly, it hit too close to home.

In Sara's youth only men got tattoos and most of them were in a branch of the armed forces and the tattoos reflected that. Nowadays, both men and women get tattoos and call them *body art*, some using their entire body as their canvas. It's no longer taboo to have multiple displays of colorful body art visible on their bodies regardless of gender.

When a person of age reacts negatively upon seeing a younger person with a colorful canvas of flesh, epithets like *senior*, *biddy*, *ancient relic*, *dinosaur*, and *golden-ager*, to name only a few of the kinder ones, can be heard. Sara didn't really have an opinion one way or another about tattoos, she felt it was a personal choice in this post-stigma tattoo era. Even if she was a young person in today's world she wouldn't choose to decorate any part of her flesh with permanent ink.

Sara decided it was time for her to make an appointment at the beauty salon. She still had the coupon for a free visit she won at her first bingo event. She made her appointment for the following Monday afternoon. She was going to have her hair returned to its natural color, cut and styled. She also scheduled a manicure. Maybe she'd get a pedicure in the coming weeks. Even at her age she refused to settle for hair of grey, silver, white or some combination of all three. She had always been a brunette with auburn highlights so she would request a muted auburn brown shade, but nothing bordering on black. Of course everyone knew an octogenarian no longer had naturally dark hair but Sara always felt she looked younger with colored hair even if it was only an illusion.

Some of the younger residents (younger by degrees; you had to be at least sixty-five years old to live at Parliament Square) were still able to drive and keep their vehicle on the premises. Although there was a sign-out and sign-in procedure in place, they could leave for short periods during the day. Limited night driving was allowed, inclement-weather driving was prohibited.

None of Sara's dining room friends had a driver's license or a vehicle. Sara thought she should have inquired around to find out who was still able to drive when she was brainstorming a way to escape after her arrival. Her desire to leave was now a distant memory; she had acclimated and, for the most part, accepted Parliament Square as her permanent home. She made new friends including Joseph, purposed herself with the daycare center volunteer work, and would soon share time with her college roommate and friend, Michele.

Sara noticed on the activities bulletin board that a karaoke night was scheduled for a week from Friday. She considered the possibilities. Jan and Betsy could team up with Pam and sing a McGuire Sisters' hit, maybe "Goodnight, Sweetheart, Goodnight," or "Sincerely," or "Sugartime," or possibly a medley of all three.

She heard Betsy and Jan singing on occasion in the hallways and they were really quite good. Sara always said that she couldn't carry a tune in a bucket, so she wasn't going to volunteer to hold a karaoke microphone in front of an audience. Maybe she would ask Joseph if he might be interested in being her date. She signed her name to the list and noted in the margin that she wanted to attend but not actively participate.

Just as she turned to leave and head for her room, Betsy and Jan came around the corner singing a show tune in perfect harmony. Sara interrupted their song to ask if they were going to attend karaoke night and if they needed a third voice for the group. As fate would have it they were on their way to sign up hoping they would be able to find a third person. Perfect! She would check with Joseph to see if he wanted to go too.

Sara knocked on Joseph's door. No answer. She knocked again and thought she heard some movement inside. She prepared to leave when the door opened and Sara saw that Joseph had apparently just awakened from a nap. He apologized for taking so long to answer and asked Sara to come in.

"Joseph, would you like to go to the karaoke night next Friday with me? I'm not going to participate but thought it would be fun to support those who are." He hesitated at first but then agreed it would be fun and he would be there. He would add his name to the list. It was a date.

Walking back to her apartment Sara crossed paths with Jean who told her that she asked Ray Adams to the Sadie Hawkins dance after learning that Joseph planned to attend with Sara. Then she filled Sara in on all the details about her newest romantic interest.

"Ray recently moved to Parliament Square after losing his wife, his driver's license and his son in a car accident. He's a very nice man who needs some support and comfort. I'm hoping to provide that for him." Sara assumed Ray was currently vulnerable which was like painting a bullseye on his back to attract Jean's attention.

"Ray and I have gone to several bingo nights together, played pinochle as a couple and are going to the Sadie Hawkins dance on Saturday. Sorry, but I have to hurry off to my appointment with Donna at the beauty salon." Her quick exit reminded Sara of an old saying: Some people light up a room when they enter, others light up a room when they leave.

Sara wanted to return to her apartment so she could call Michele to ask about her arrival date at Parliament Square. It was already the first week of November and Sara thought Michele should be here. She hoped nothing had changed her decision to move in.

The phone rang and rang but no answer. Sara left a message asking Michele to call her back. With the receiver still in her hand, Sara thought back to the day she met Michele at college. That had been many, many years ago but the memory remained crystal clear.

It was move-in weekend for new freshmen and Sara, with her mother, stepfather, and a pile of her belongings, was ready to begin her college education to become a registered nurse. She had been assigned to a third-floor room in the Walker Building and upon entering the two-person room that only provided enough space for one, Sara met her roommate, Michele.

Michele was black. Sara had little history with anyone who wasn't white and she had no black friends. Although Sara wasn't opposed to having a black roommate, her mother wasn't happy about it. She wanted to go to the dean of students and change room assignments immediately.

The *Brown v. Board of Education* decision, reached several months earlier, removed the ability of states to control segregation in public schools. It had started a movement for equality regardless of race or color. Sara and her class in Ireland had followed it closely.

She explained to her mother that she wanted to be roommates with Michele and learn black culture firsthand. Sara's mother was adamant about changing, but her stepfather, much to her surprise, sided with Sara. There would be no changes. Michele and Sara would be roommates and, as it turned out, friends for life.

Sara's eyelids grew heavy and she drifted off into a *what if* moment...

The day has finally arrived. After a year of extensive counseling I have come to terms with the loss of Andrew and the baby. I'm so excited to begin my college education. My mother and stepfather decide that, although I could commute to campus, it would be better if I lived there. It would save time that I can use to focus on my studies.

I also think they want me out of the house so they can focus on all of Barbie's activities. But that's just my opinion. I'm actually on board with living on campus as it will expand my horizons, reduce parental monitoring, and allow more independent thinking and decision making.

We unload my belongings into my third-floor dorm. It's a small, recently painted room with two windows that look out onto the adjoining building. Not much of a view, but I'll be too busy studying to admire a scenic vista anyhow.

I've been assigned a roommate but all I know is that she's from Atlanta and her name is Michele. She's also a freshman; housing is assigned by academic year. When I arrive, much to my surprise, I see a black woman making up the bed on the right side of the room. At first I think she might be an employee but when she turns around and introduces herself as Michele my heart sinks. I realize that I've stereotyped her based on the color of her skin.

She is my roommate, not the maid. My mother turns pale as a ghost and asks that I please step into the hallway for a moment where she tells me that we are immediately going to the dean of students and having this situation remedied. She insists that I room with a white student and although I tell her that I don't want to be assigned a different room-mate, I'm reassigned to a different room anyway.

We retrieve my belongings and I move to another room in the same building. I'm upset and unhappy with the reassignment but both my mother and stepfather demand it. I see Michele in passing but we never bond as we would have had we been roommates and I regret my mother's decision to have me reassigned.

Knock...knock...knock..."Housekeeping"...knock... knock. Sara opened her eyes, slowly walked to the door, and was met by Pearl, a woman of color, who had been assigned to clean Sara's apartment today. How ironic that after all these years certain positions in life still seem to be compartmentalized by skin color. So much has changed since those college days in the fifties and yet so much has stayed the same.

Sara decided to keep the recurring *what if* moments to herself. It worried Michael when she told him about the first couple of times it happened. She rather enjoyed the moments, seeing how possible alternate life choices could have impacted her life. She felt it was her mind's way of transporting her to *what-could-have-been* situations. She found it intriguing but sometimes also a bit frightening.

It was November eighteenth, the day of the Sadie Hawkins dance. Sara awoke to the sound of people talking. She tried to determine where the voices were coming from and eventually realized that Penelope had apparently stepped on the television remote and she was listening to the morning news. Whew, that was a relief. She thought maybe she was hearing voices in her head or, worse, it was the voice of a higher power calling her home.

Sara made an appointment with Donna to have her hair styled that day at ten o'clock in preparation for the night's festivities. She also picked out one of her favorite dresses and shoes that were comfortable with a small heel and in no way orthopedic in style. She may have to kick them off when seated at the table but they would certainly be a step up from her normal athletic shoe or orthotic insert flat.

ELAINE C. BAUMBACH

She had breakfast and coffee in her apartment that morning and relaxed a bit before her appointment with Donna. She
missed the camaraderie of sharing breakfast with her dining
companions. She had learned to accept her new friends, her
daily schedule, the planned activities and even to some degree
being "pampered," aka monitored, by the staff.

Sara's hair appointment was a success and she felt a bit
of outer beauty which, at her age, was sometimes difficult
if not impossible to achieve. People can be beautiful inside
forever, but their outward appearance, which was too often
how others judged them, was negatively impacted by wrinkles, gravity-induced sagging, varicose and spider veins, dark
spots, arthritic bone deformities, and the list went on and on.
Sara thought of the saying *beauty is only skin deep*. Those of
advanced age certainly hope there is truth in it.

Inside many people in their seventies, eighties, nineties or older lives a younger spirit asking how they got this
old and looking for an escape route. Younger people assume
that seniors think older, different thoughts. If those younger
people are lucky enough to reach their golden years, they will
understand that often the thought process doesn't age at the
same rate as the physical body. There are exceptions to that, of
course, for those whose minds are afflicted with dementia or
Alzheimer's, but barring that, most feel a great deal younger in
their heads than they look on the outside.

After the evening meal, those who planned to attend
the Sadie Hawkins dance were asked to return to the activity room at seven o'clock. Volunteers from a local Girl Scout
troop spent the afternoon decorating the room with streamers, helium balloons and colorful decorations.

An employee of Parliament Square would be the DJ for the
night playing records from the forties, fifties and sixties. All
were encouraged to attend whether they had invited someone
or not. There would be light refreshments and a photo booth

so that couples could document the evening in pictures. It was going to be a fun evening.

Some married couples were in attendance; the wives invited their husbands to escort them to the event. As mentioned on the sign-up sheet because female residents outnumbered the men, women should feel free to invite other women, so there were some two-woman couples.

When Joseph, in a preppy looking outfit sporting a blue button-down Oxford shirt, navy blue blazer and penny loafers, entered the room with Sara on his arm they heard several people whisper what a "cute" couple they made. Sara felt the eyes of the room on her and for a brief moment forgot that she was in her eighties. She thought she saw a special twinkle in Joseph's blue eyes that wasn't there before.

Jean and her date, Ray Adams, stopped to exchange pleasantries with Sara and Joseph. Sara thought Ray looked familiar but couldn't remember where she'd seen him. Maybe it would come to her later.

The photo booth was fun. Joseph and Sara made some silly faces while wearing oversized colorful glasses, feather boas and crazy hats. Any troubles and cares were erased, at least for the evening, while they allowed themselves to be transported to happier, younger times. These pictures would certainly be refrigerator magnet worthy.

The music played, the couples danced, and it was certainly an evening to remember. Unlike David, who never liked to dance, Joseph enjoyed it and, for him, the moves were smooth and effortless.

Joseph confided, "My wife coerced me into taking dance lessons early in our marriage. I never regretted having the Arthur Murray dance instructors teach me the classic steps. At the time I was against it but it turned out to be a very good decision. Instead of being afraid of the dance floor I really enjoy it."

The DJ played an assortment of music. Some songs had a jitterbug tempo, some allowed the dancers to showcase their individual version of the stroll and some had a perfect tempo for the classic slow dance which allowed you to hold your partner close and gracefully dip to the music.

The last song of the evening was Frankie Laine's 1953 hit "I Believe." How appropriate...a perfect slow dance to end a perfect evening.

Chapter Thirteen: Reunion

location, location, location

Is it possible to awaken with a smile on your face? Sara felt that is just what she did the morning after the Sadie Hawkins dance. She may have been smiling all through the night.

Maybe she should have a mirror installed over her bed so she could look up to see if she was smiling in the morning. No, wait, having a mirror over her bed could be misinterpreted! The mere thought of that made her laugh out loud. An octogenarian with a mirror on the ceiling could make the *Parliament Square Times*, but not for the right reasons. Okay, enough silly thoughts for one morning.

She hardly noticed the normal arthritic aches and pains as she walked to the bathroom. Maybe it was because she had taken a double dose of her medication before the dance. Whatever it was, she felt better than she had in a long, long time.

She felt so comfortable and safe in Joseph's arms. It had been over five years since she lost her precious David and, with the exception of a couple of male suitors since then, none of whom had piqued her interest, she had almost forgotten the feeling of having a significant other. Not that she and Joseph were more than two retirement village neighbors at this point in time. In her heart she felt that maybe, just maybe, this could be the start of something more.

Sara basked in the afterglow of the previous evening's diary-eligible moments when the telephone sharply brought her back to reality. It was Michele. "Sara, my move-in date has been finalized and it's December the 11th, three Mondays after Thanksgiving. Final details are still being worked out. As it turns out there's a unit on the third floor right down the hall from you. I've been on a waiting list for an opening, which is why I haven't moved in already. I can't wait for us to spend some time together like the good old days. I'm so glad that you'll be there for me."

This retirement village was one of the highest rated facilities in the area and was currently in the process of adding another building which would house an additional forty to fifty residents. The average life expectancy was constantly increasing. The need for senior housing outnumbered the availability, causing longer than average wait times.

Michele told Sara, "I'll be coming on Monday or Tuesday to have a tour, eat lunch with the residents and see the apartment I'll be moving into. I'll ask if we could have lunch together."

Sara replied, "I'll be sure to eat lunch in the dining room on Monday and Tuesday and will look for you. You don't have to ask anyone's permission to have lunch with me. I can't wait to see you." After a bit more conversation, they said goodbye and Sara went to the kitchen to make coffee.

She was too comfortable in her robe and jammies to think about rushing to get ready for breakfast in the dining room. She would enjoy a quiet cup of coffee and some cinnamon sugar toast with Penelope this morning. The chilly November wind howled outside the window, but inside her apartment and her heart it was warm and cozy.

Sara was still in her robe at ten o'clock when someone knocked on her door. She almost declined to answer because she didn't feel presentable. Through the peephole she saw a young man she didn't recognize. "Who's there?" she asked.

"I have a delivery for Sara Jennings."

Sara slowly opened the door and the young man handed her a box tied with a big red ribbon. She thanked him, took the box to the kitchen and placed it on the counter.

Penelope jumped up to investigate. Sara opened the card. It was from Joseph. "Thank you for a wonderful evening and for helping me begin to understand life can go on after losing my precious Theresa. You are a very special lady!" Sara opened the box to find beautiful long-stemmed roses.

Tears welled in her eyes. She was touched and honored that Joseph sent her flowers with such a beautifully written heartfelt message. With Penelope's assistance, she arranged the flowers in a vase and enveloped herself in their beauty. She couldn't remember the last time she had received flowers. She wanted them to last forever.

The dinner conversation for the week focused on karaoke night. Jan and Betsy encouraged Pam to be the third McGuire sister and, after some consideration and rehearsing, she agreed. They were going to present a medley of McGuire Sisters hits, singing the first several verses of each song. They decided to wear black slacks, white blouses and make their hair look as big as reasonably possible.

They could be found practicing in the activity room most evenings. Sara was impressed by how good they sounded. Not everyone was born with a singing voice, but these three women all were.

Most of her tablemates would be attending with the exception of Mary, who was still quite upset about her daughter's health issues, and Deborah who apparently had other plans. Of course, Jim had a bit of music humor to share with his tablemates: "Middle C, E-flat and G walk into a bar. 'Sorry,' the bartender says to the E-flat, 'we don't serve minors here.'" Several moans were heard and although Pam found it extremely funny, she managed to keep all the food she was chewing inside her mouth.

Joseph and Sara arrived at the karaoke event early hoping to get two seats close to the makeshift stage. Sara could hear Betsy, Jan and Pam warming up in the adjoining room. Jim was elected by the residents to be the announcer for the evening. Surely he would have some humorous moments and comments to share with the audience as the activities progressed. The first singer was scheduled to begin at eight o'clock.

The seats filled up as the starting time approached. There was talk that one of the residents was going to do his Elvis impersonation. Cindy walked to the microphone. "Can everyone please be seated as the first singer is about to start the program. Please hold your applause until the song is over." She then turned the microphone over to Jim. The audience chanted Jim's name and clapped their hands in unison. The show was about to begin.

The first several songs were really quite enjoyable and nostalgic of days gone by. It was much better than today's music, but every generation thinks that. At least the lyrics were recognizable words and phrases which is not the case with modern-day songs. Sara often tried to determine what the lyrics of today's popular songs were when she heard them but was unable to do so.

The McGuire Sisters' medley performed by Betsy, Jan and Pam proved to be the hit of the evening. They really sounded quite professional and even did some synchronized movements, Pam using her bedazzled walker, during the singing. The crowd was on their feet when they finished, shouting *Encore! Encore! Encore!* They sang one more McGuire Sisters song and then they waved and exited the stage.

Jim announced, "This concludes the program for the evening and in closing I want to ask why the pianist kept banging his head against the keys. Drum roll please...he was playing by ear." There were audible groans and, if it's even possible, audible eye rolls.

Refreshments were served in the dining room following the program. Joseph and Sara decided to stop by for some freshly made popcorn and punch. Jan and Betsy were flying high after their stellar performance. Sara asked them for their autographs. They shared a laugh about that.

Pam decided to skip the refreshments and retire for the evening. All that performing made her tired. Sara thought to

135

herself how glad she was that she had decided to participate in the activities instead of isolating herself in her room, where she would still be sad, alone and depressed, just as she was during her first months at Parliament Square.

There were residents in that same situation today and Sara wanted to give each of them a pep talk about getting involved and creating their own happiness. It's not possible to force someone to be happy. They must learn that true happiness comes from within and not from external sources.

Saturday morning seemed to arrive sooner than usual. Michael would be in the lobby at ten o'clock to pick her up. Sara had so much she wanted to share with him. She wrote several items on a piece of paper and slipped it into her purse. Now she just had to remember to get the list out of her purse when they were together.

Michael had called earlier in the week suggesting that she wear something warm since they may stop at the cemetery, weather permitting. Sara hoped they were going to do that. She wanted to talk to David about her new friend, Joseph. She was sure he would approve.

The day with Michael went by so quickly. They visited the cemetery where Michael gave Aunt Sara some alone time with David, asking her to keep it brief because the wind was quite brisk and he didn't want her getting chilled. She talked to David about her date with Joseph on Sadie Hawkins Day and attending the karaoke event together but she omitted the part about the roses because she didn't want to upset him. Then she bade him farewell for today and blew him a kiss as she headed for the car.

Michael planned lunch at a new restaurant that served fish and chips, which happened to be a favorite of Aunt Sara's. She remembered to get out her list of items to discuss and they talked about every one of them over lunch. Michael was so glad to hear that his aunt and Joseph were enjoying each other's company, that Michele was soon moving in and that Aunt Sara really felt purposeful helping in the daycare center.

Michael said, "You've come a long way in a short period of time and I'm really proud of you. When I see you like this I know we made the right decision, as difficult as it may have been. Having Joseph and Michele there to spend your time with is wonderful." Their day together ended too soon but Sara enjoyed it while it lasted.

Thanksgiving dinner at Parliament Square was open to family and friends. Michael planned to spend the day with his wife Marcy and some friends, which was fine with Sara. She was excited because Michele, her daughter and her daughter's family were coming.

Michele hadn't been able to come for lunch the previous week as she was under the weather with a touch of the flu, but fortunately she was better in time for Thanksgiving. Sara would sit with Michele and her family for the feast. Joseph went to his daughter's house, so Sara looked forward to spending some time with Michele.

The dinner was quite good and after dessert Sara suggested that Michele come with her to see her unit and visit with Penelope. They were so glad to be reunited after not seeing each other since Sara had moved away. Michele was a bit apprehensive about the impending move, as Sara had been when she first arrived, but Michele had the advantage of knowing a current resident quite well, so she might not feel so isolated and totally alone.

It would be hard leaving her longtime home where she had raised her daughter but Michele had some mobility issues which made stairs challenging and dangerous for her. Relatives, friends and an in-home services company helped her with daily activities but the time had come to move to a more secure location where there were no steps, yardwork or household maintenance.

She was in a much better frame of mind than Sara was on her first day. They would have the same address again just like they had during their college days, but this time they would be hallmates, not roommates.

When Michele and her family departed for the day, Sara returned to her apartment to relax. She turned on the television and made herself comfortable on the bed. She closed her eyes for a moment.

She thought about how she and David almost didn't buy the cottage by the sea. She remembered them going to see another house that wasn't located on the ocean. They liked it and told the realtor that they needed to discuss it before making an offer. The realtor said that he had shown the house to several others and felt one of them would make an offer soon. Their guess was that realtors tell every prospective buyer that same story in an effort to close the sale.

David loved the large yard and the fact that he would have a short commute to work. Sara loved that it was in move-in condition and would need little more than some cosmetic changes. They decided to grab a bite on the way home and talk about it in more detail. They made a list of pros and cons with the pros a definite winner. They decided to sleep on it and call the realtor in the morning to make an offer.

Unfortunately, as fate would have it, they received a call around midnight notifying them that David's mother had been rushed to the hospital with an apparent heart attack. David jumped out of bed, dressed and drove to the hospital immediately.

He arrived too late. His mother was pronounced dead before he could get there to say his goodbyes. David had been an only child so he had to take charge of the funeral arrangements, notify all the relatives, write the obituary, plan the wake, etc. Sara assisted him as much as possible, but he took the loss very hard. He and his mother had been incredibly close.

Funeral activities consumed the next week. By the time they called the realtor to make their offer they were told that the house had been sold. David was dreadfully disappointed. Sara was too but she still had her heart set on a home by the water.

Several weeks later they went to see the beautiful cottage by the sea, and the rest is history. If not for the unfortunate timing of David's mother's death they would never have seen the cottage that became their home for decades. Maybe they would have been as happy in the other house but that is something they would never know.

The years evaporated and Sara became enveloped in a *what if* moment. It seemed so long ago yet it also seemed like it was just yesterday.

David asked me several times to please be ready on time. The real estate agent will be here any minute. He knows that I'm occasionally a bit tardy for appointments. If you look up the word punctuality *in the dictionary, you'll see David's picture there. His pet peeve is being late himself, or others being late. I tell him I understand what time the agent is arriving and I'll be ready by then.*

This is a very important day for us. We are saving our money and have been for several years. We want to buy our first house as a married couple and one has come on the market that we are awfully interested in seeing. I want to live on the coast, maybe even on the beach, but David would rather reside in town closer to work, restaurants and social venues. This house is a bit of a compromise as it's on the outskirts of town and close to the water but not directly on the beach.

We drive to the house with the realtor and have a walk-through of the property. It is in great condition and we are told that the owner is selling because her husband recently passed away and she can no longer take care of the house alone. It's a bittersweet moment as we are extremely excited to be starting our life's journey together here, while the woman is sad to be leaving the home where she and her husband made so many memories together. Life can be that way. As Albert Einstein put it, "Learn from yesterday, live for today, hope for tomorrow."

Life happens and with it comes twists and turns that can generate very different results, some to which we are totally oblivious. Life has no rear-view mirror. We look straight ahead to see what's coming toward us, not behind to see what could have been.

We immediately put a deposit on the house, our offer is accepted and we are able to move in within weeks. We never see the cottage by the sea and we live our life together in this house with no ocean view, never knowing what we missed. They say timing is everything. It all comes down to being at the right place at the right time.

Sara awakened and found that she had dozed off for two hours. That flashback memory of house hunting with David was so fresh in her mind it felt like it just happened.

As Sara advanced in age she understood that life was no longer the same as it once was. Yet on occasion she felt that time had not passed and she was still that same younger person inside, even though her outer appearance contradicted that thinking.

She had recently watched a program discussing the many paranormal television shows and movies depicting vampires and situations that are likely outside the realm of reality. Realizing the lack of credibility in those stories but still getting so involved in them that logical thinking is suspended in order to believe they are true is called *suspension of disbelief.* Sara wondered if realizing she had aged but still believing a younger Sara dwelled inside of her aged body could be called *unsuspended belief.*

Chapter Fourteen: Disappointment

tragedy

At the dinner table on the Sunday following Thanksgiving, Mary tapped her water glass with her spoon loudly, which was totally out of character. "May I have your attention please? I will be leaving Parliament Square tomorrow. I waited until the last minute to tell you because I have mixed emotions about my decision. I'm going to live with my daughter and her family in Florida. It's a difficult time for everyone and I want to help in any way I can.

"I moved to Parliament Square by choice after losing my husband. It was just too hard to live alone in the home we shared through so many years. Every corner of the residence held memories we made together and living there without him was like no pain I have ever experienced. It was sometimes so intense I couldn't explain it. There are no words to express what I felt. Those of you who have lost a spouse understand what I'm trying to say.

"At that time my daughter asked me to come live with her and her family in Florida but I declined. I didn't want to be a burden. It sounds good on the surface but it is a definite invasion of privacy."

Mary went on. "Now that she has advanced breast cancer and an intense treatment plan she needs me much more than I needed a place to live. I offered to come and she accepted. She wants me there to help her during this difficult time.

"Who knows what the future holds for any of us? I may return some day but for now I need to be with her." That was the most that Mary had ever shared. Hugs were exchanged, prayers were said, and some tears were shed. The table was definitely going to miss Mary's quiet, poised demeanor.

The week appeared to be taking a downward turn. First Mary's announcement that she was leaving Parliament Square and then, on Tuesday evening, a call from Michael which was even more upsetting. "Aunt Sara," he started, "I've been offered a promotion. It's a lot more money and a vice presidency. I'll have to move to California for at least the next twelve months. After that I may be able to return but nothing is definite at this point except that I must move to California after Christmas."

Sara put on a good façade telling him that she was so excited to hear his good news. Inside she was especially sad that he would be away for a year or more, which translated into no Saturdays together, and he would not be here for special events. She felt self-centered and selfish having those feelings in light of his promotion and made every effort to be upbeat and supportive during their conversation.

When the call ended, Sara started crying and couldn't stop. She hadn't cried in some time and hoped the tears would be soul cleansing, but instead they just made her nose run and her eyes turn bloodshot. She cuddled Penelope for comfort and made her promise to never leave her, as if a cat is even capable of doing such a thing.

Sara saw Cindy in the lobby the next day and asked, "Has a replacement been chosen to sit at our dining room table since Mary's departure? A very good friend of mine from college is moving in soon and I wondered if she could be Mary's replacement."

Cindy replied, "I'll mention that to the people in charge of seating. I have no ability to make that happen, but I can certainly pass it along."

When a resident moved away to another location or was called home by a higher power, their seat in the dining room was vacated and the powers that be decided if a current resident would be assigned to that seat or if the seat would be left open until a new resident arrived. It would be perfect if Michele's arrival coincided with the assignment of Mary's replacement. Sitting with Michele would boost Sara's spirits and provide her with a relationship like the one that Jan and Betsy have, of which she must admit she was quite envious.

Moving day for Michele arrived and Sara placed a Christmas wreath on the door to Michele's apartment prior to her arrival. The other residents planned their Christmas visits with family and friends. Michael will be spending Christmas with Sara before heading to California.

He traveled to the West Coast early in December. He was picking Sara up Christmas Eve and she would spend the night and the following day with Michael and his wife, Marcy. She had never connected with Marcy over the years that she and Michael have been married.

Marcy tends to be a private woman, lacking warmth and sociability. That's not to say she isn't a nice person, but getting past her hard exterior can be challenging if not impossible. She doesn't seem jealous of Michael's relationship with Sara, but neither is she supportive of their family bond.

Sara would never have matched Michael with Marcy; she saw them as a definite mismatch of personalities from the start. But Michael seems happy enough with their relationship, so who was she to question it? Sara's sister, Barb, had confided in her when her health was failing that she never approved of Michael's marriage to Marcy. Barb felt that Marcy was a gold digger and that she married Michael because of his potential for success and his family's wealth. She felt the relationship would crumble, but it hadn't yet.

Time came for the evening meal on Michele's move-in day and Sara was disappointed to see Michele seated at a table on the other side of the room. Just then one of the Parliament Square attendants walked Michele over to Sara's table and said that Michele had seated herself in the wrong place. This was her new home for mealtimes. Everyone at the table stood and welcomed her to the group. Sara beamed as she introduced everyone to Michele, her old friend from college.

Sara invited Michele to come sit with her in the lobby area after dinner. The two sat on a comfortable floral-print upholstered couch and chatted away like they had never been separated. Time apart does not negatively impact those with friendships dating back to much earlier times in their lives.

Friends who establish that younger-in-life bond can go long periods of time without seeing or talking to each other, but when they next meet they can pick up right where they left off months, years or even decades before.

It seems that early bonds of friendship run deep within the soul and almost permeate our genetic structure. Having a friend for life is a gift. Losing a friend for life is a tragedy. In the words of Winnie the Pooh, "If you live to be 100, I hope I live to be 100 minus a day, so I never have to live without you."

Sara and Michele took the elevator together to the third floor, hugged and wished each other a good night's sleep. They've been afforded the ability to reconnect and not only share precious memories from their past but also make new memories together in their twilight years. What a true blessing.

Although Michael would be far away for a while, she now had Michele and Joseph in her life to alleviate the painful loss she felt with his impending departure. Maybe it was divine intervention that they had been placed in her life at this moment in time when she needed them the most.

Sara and Joseph made plans to play pinochle with another couple after dinner one evening. With Thanksgiving, Michele moving in and Michael's news about moving, they hadn't spent much time together in the absence of others.

The card game was fun and Sara began to understand her attraction to Joseph. He possessed many of the same personality traits that David did. Although there were no similarities in their physical appearance, there were many likenesses in demeanor, values and behavior. Sara never thought she would meet a man who would mirror David in so many ways. In her heart she felt a strong affection developing for Joseph and she had no intention of fighting those feelings.

Christmas was fast approaching. Michael told Aunt Sara not to buy him any presents. Their celebrating the holiday together would be her gift to him. He said that maybe she could fly out for a visit after he settled in but she wasn't comfortable flying anymore. Maybe she would change her mind, but more than likely she wouldn't.

Joseph was going to spend the holiday with his daughter and her family. Michele would go to her daughter's house. The Christmas holiday remained difficult for Sara since David passed away. They had created so many traditions over the years and celebrating without him left a void in the festivities.

She understood that traditions were good, so enjoyable and looked forward to by many, but when one of those helping to create and celebrate the tradition was no longer there neither was the joyful celebration of the event. That was one of the hardest adjustments for Sara to make since losing David, no longer being able to celebrate events that had relevance to them as a couple.

The Saturday before Christmas arrived and many residents were leaving with relatives for a long weekend or getting ready to leave on the following day, which was Christmas Eve. At the dinner table that night Michele, Pam and Deborah were missing as they had already left for the holiday weekend. Joseph, Sara, Jan and Betsy were leaving to be with family the next day. Jim was the only resident at the table who was staying at Parliament Square for the holiday. He had no relatives in the area. There would be a Christmas dinner on Monday for those who weren't spending the holiday with family.

Dinner conversation centered on the events each person would be attending or the traditions they would be celebrating with their families. Holidays can be a challenging time for younger folks but they can be an especially difficult time for

147

people of age who have no family with whom to celebrate. It is especially hard for those who used to have family but no longer did. The absence of those loved ones leaves a huge void that's very hard to fill at special holiday times.

Sara and Joseph sat together in the lobby after dinner that night. They talked about childhood Christmas memories, family traditions, and their impending weekend plans. Sara thought about how effortless her conversations with Joseph were. He was such a nice man and also quite handsome.

Joseph asked, "Sara, do you plan to attend the New Year's party?"

She replied, "I might consider attending if the right gentleman were to invite me."

"Well, I hope that happens. It would be a shame to miss the party." They both laughed and agreed that they would like to ring in the New Year together although neither could guarantee they would still be awake at midnight. She had rung in the New Year many, many times but this year was going to be special. She could feel it in her osteopenia-riddled bones.

That night in her bed, without the overhead mirror, the thought of which still made her laugh, Sara let her mind wander to Christmases past. She and David would always attend the candlelight Christmas Eve service at church. They would return home to cuddle in front of the fireplace while watching the antique bubble lights on the Christmas tree illuminate the otherwise dark room. They would exchange one present before midnight and retire for the evening. It was a simple celebration, but one they both agreed was perfect.

After she lost David, she would still go to church, sit in front of the fireplace watching the bubble lights and retire for the evening missing David more than any other day of the year. This would be the first Christmas in over forty years she would not be in the cottage by the sea and she did feel a bit sad about that but she encouraged herself to savor the wonderful memories and replace the sadness she felt with gratitude for what she had and for what was yet to come.

She vividly remembered answering the door that cold January night to find a state policeman standing on the other side, his vehicle parked in the driveway with the lights flashing. At first she had no idea why he was there, possibly to warn her about a burglary in the neighborhood, maybe to sell her tickets for a charity event, or to inform her of an escaped convict in the area. Their annual mid-winter party was just getting started so it couldn't be for disturbing the peace. It never crossed her mind to even imagine it was because David had been involved in a traffic accident. He was such a safe driver, always cautious, always abiding by the speed limits, and most of all always wearing his seat belt.

The officer told her that David's vehicle had been hit by a suspected drunk driver, forced off the road and down a steep embankment. Upon hitting the bottom the car had burst into flames and there was nothing that could be done to assist David. He more than likely died on impact and was consumed by the explosion and fire. Her David was gone. If only he had listened to her and not gone out to buy balloons.

Even now, almost five years later, that memory reared its ugly head. She was overwhelmed with grief. Why did it have to happen? How can life be so unfair?

She had come to terms with losing David on most days, but occasionally she fell back into a grief that seemed as painful as the day of the accident. She had a good cry, which usually helped calm her, and she thought back to their last Christmas together and the good times they shared over their decades of marriage. She blew her nose, which attracted Penelope's attention, and she came over and lay next to Sara as if trying to comfort her.

As slumber enveloped Sara's thoughts she was transported to one of the saddest times in her life, losing her beloved David. But *what if...*

"David, I think we have all the supplies for our party tomorrow evening. I made a list and checked it twice and then once more," Sara called out to David. Each year in late January, David and I host a mid-winter event for friends and family in an effort to break up the winter doldrums after the holidays have passed. The cold Massachusetts winter weather and short, dark days are cause enough for a reason to throw a party.

All that's left of the Christmas holidays are the credit card bills and the unwanted gifts that remain to be "regifted" to some unsuspecting soul next year. The event boasts lots of food, adult beverages and games. We love to play games like Pictionary, Trivial Pursuit, charades and even Twister. It's a fun evening and it often becomes a sleepover unless there are designated drivers to take our inebriated friends home for the night.

Late in the afternoon, before the party, as we put the finishing touches on the night's preparations, David asks me where the balloons are for the pass-the-balloon-to-your-partner-without-dropping-it game. I rummage through a couple of drawers and tell him I can't find any but we can skip that game this year. He tells me that he has time to run out and pick some up. I tell him because we have so many other games to play no one will miss the balloon game. He begrudgingly agrees and soon after the first guests begin to arrive.

We continue to host the mid-winter January event into our eighties. This year's event will have fewer participants, many with less flexibility and slower responses to the word or memory games. The cottage by the sea welcomes our guests each year as it has over the past decades. How much longer we will be able to host is uncertain, but for now, with help from family and friends, we celebrate another needed break from the winter doldrums. I am especially looking forward to the Twister game. Last year it took three people to untangle the geriatric participants.

When Sara awoke the next morning she noticed tear stains on her pillowcase. She still mourned her precious David. He lost his life on an unnecessary trip to the store for balloons. For a long time after the fatal accident Sara blamed herself for not finding the balloons in the basement or for not insisting that David forget about going out to get them.

She eventually found peace when she accepted the fact that it was David's time, so whether it had been on a trip to the store for balloons or during a walk on the beach or lying silently asleep in bed next to her; he would have been called home. Although her *what if* moment didn't support that thinking, Sara truly believed that everyone had an invisible expiration date stamped on them at birth. The only way a mortal can alter that date is through self-destruction. It's all part of a much higher master plan for which the blueprints are divine.

Chapter Fifteen: Tradition

indiscretion / forgiveness

Christmas Eve arrived with a fresh coating of snow. Sara hoped the storm didn't bring too much as she looked forward to Michael picking her up to celebrate Christmas. She had taken the Parliament Square van to the mall a couple of weeks ago and picked out gifts for Michael and Marcy. Michael discouraged any exchange of gifts, Sara refused to go empty handed.

She purchased a warm cashmere scarf in dark grey for Michael. It was a bit pricey but she could afford it and he had helped her so much over the past year. After much deliberation Sara decided on some nice warm gloves and a matching hat in a neutral color with a well-known designer label for Marcy, although she doubted the gift would be received with much enthusiasm. Marcy normally exhibited about as much excitement as a hibernating bear in January.

The breakfast table was almost empty that morning. Jim was there as were Betsy and Jan. Joseph, Pam, Deborah and Michele had already departed for the holiday weekend. Jim, despite the fact that he had no family to celebrate with him, was in good spirits. Some people are blessed with the ability to put a positive spin on situations that cause others anxiety and sadness. Jim was one of those people.

He shared several jokes made famous by comedian George Burns who lived to the ripe old age of 100. The first was, "People ask me what I'd most appreciate getting for my 87th birthday. I tell them a paternity suit." The second was, "Happiness is having a large, loving, caring, close-knit family in another city." The third was, "Old age is when you resent the swimsuit issue of Sports Illustrated because there are fewer articles to read." The fourth and final joke was, "When I was a boy, the Dead Sea was only sick."

The few who were at the table clapped and wished Jim a Merry Christmas as they left the dining room to prepare for the holiday.

Sara went to say good-bye to Penelope who had to stay behind because Marcy was allergic to cats (Sara doubted it was true). A staff member would check on Penelope for the next couple of days and feed her in Sara's absence.

She double checked her suitcase to be sure she hadn't forgotten anything, hugged Penelope, locked the door and headed for the elevator. She looked forward to celebrating Christmas with Michael before he left for California.

She saw Jim in the lobby. "Merry Christmas. I hope you enjoy the celebration here. See you in a couple of days," she said as she gave him a big hug. She sat on the sofa by the window so she could watch for Michael's arrival. Fortunately, the snow had subsided and the forecast was all clear for the next several days. When Michael arrived, he took Aunt Sara's suitcase and held her by the arm, escorting her across the slippery sidewalk to the car. He always took such good care of his Aunt Sara. She was going to miss him a lot!

The trip to Michael's house took about a half hour which gave them time to share what was going on in each other's lives. Michael was extremely excited about his promotion and the impending move to the West Coast. He said, "Marcy isn't totally supportive of the move and has threatened to stay in Massachusetts. We discussed it and she agreed to give it a try, but if she doesn't like it in two or three months, she'll come back east. I'm not sure how that's going to work out."

Sara thought that the best thing that could happen to Michael would be to lose Marcy, even temporarily, but she certainly wouldn't share that with him. She said, "Joseph and I made plans to ring in the New Year together. He sent me beautiful roses with a lovely note attached." Michael didn't remind her that she had already told him that when they talked on the phone last week. Sometimes the aging process causes people to repeat themselves unintentionally and it's polite for younger listeners to avoid pointing it out. Someday they may also be guilty of the same behavior.

When they arrived at Michael's place it was mid-morning. He asked, "Aunt Sara, please be especially quiet. Marcy is sleeping late today. She's not a morning person and she likes to get some extra sleep on the weekends. I, on the other hand, am a morning person and rarely stay in bed later than eight even if I have the opportunity to do so. We're all either morning people or night people. I guess Marcy and I are mismatched when it comes to that." Sara thought they were incompatible in many more ways than sleep patterns.

Sara had always been a morning person and now later in life had difficulty sleeping past seven o'clock and Penelope often encouraged her to get up even earlier. She thought that lounging in bed was a waste of valuable time. She wondered how some people could get up, have breakfast and return to bed until lunchtime, or how others stay in their jammies all day, taking naps and waking long enough to eat, read a book or watch a show on television. But who was she to judge others, especially retirees who started each day with a clean slate.

Sara left her shoes at the front door, a rule that Marcy strictly enforced. Wearing street shoes in the house was not an option. She had other rules too that sometimes made Sara feel uncomfortable. Michael abided by the "Marcy Rules" but Sara sensed he didn't approve.

Sometimes people spend their life in a marriage that looks normal on the surface, but further scrutiny exposes flaws, like a cracked foundation, dangerous and in need of repair. Some are content to live in disrepair while others explore options for restoration. Sara feared that Michael and Marcy's marriage could crumble, as her sister had phrased it, at any time. Maybe this move to the West Coast would show Michael what life could be like without the burden of living with Marcy.

Christmas Eve was quiet but enjoyable. They didn't attend any evening church services, which Sara missed, but they did have a nice fire to warm them and a beautifully decorated tree to share. Sara was glad that she was able to celebrate the holiday away from Parliament Square, with family.

Choosing not to have children allowed Sara and David lots of free time and money to use for travel or high-ticket items or expensive dinners. There were no college savings accounts to fund, braces to buy, or simply the everyday expenses of raising a child. However, the other side of that coin was that in old age there weren't any grown adult children to depend on for support, guidance and companionship. Fortunately, Sara had Michael, her deceased younger sister's son—her nephew—for most of those things.

On Christmas morning they enjoyed a leisurely breakfast which Michael prepared (he did the bulk of the cooking), exchanged Christmas gifts and discussed plans for the rest of the day. Marcy's parents lived in Texas but didn't like to fly so they were never around for the holidays. She was the only child of a Lutheran minister and a music teacher. Her parents were now both retired and loved to spend time working in their garden, landscaping and playing bridge.

Marcy normally visited them once or twice a year as her work schedule permitted. From outward appearances, Marcy and her parents didn't seem to have a close family bond. Many times over the years, when Marcy was away visiting her parents, Sara and Michael would plan activities together. It seemed to her that Michael almost looked forward to Marcy being away.

Sara had an uneasy feeling in the pit of her stomach and it wasn't caused by the breakfast sausage. This marriage had the structural strength of a house of cards. She wanted to talk with Michael about it but Michael was a grown man and she didn't want to stick her nose where it didn't belong. For now, she would hold her tongue and remain silent.

Early on Tuesday morning, the day after Christmas, Michael packed Aunt Sara's suitcase into the trunk of his car and they started the thirty-minute trip back to Parliament Square. The two days had passed quickly and it was time for Michael to prepare for his trip west. Sara said thank you and goodbye to Marcy on Christmas night before going to bed since Marcy made it quite clear that she had no intention of awakening early to say farewell. Michael could do so much better.

The ride home was quiet. They had little left to discuss after spending the last two days together. Sara reminded him to call her when he was settled in his new apartment. She missed him already and he was sitting right next to her. She always felt so safe and content when she was in his company.

Michael helped Aunt Sara up to her room before kissing her on the forehead, saying goodbye to Penelope and telling her to take good care of herself. She felt a bit melancholy at that moment. Christmas was over for another year and the date of her wedding anniversary with David was fast approaching.

They had chosen New Year's Eve to get married, David said, so they could file their income taxes for that year as a married couple and get the higher standard deduction. That wasn't the truth but it made for a good story over their forty-seven years of marriage. Sara wasn't exactly sure how they arrived at that wedding date but remembers saying that getting married on New Year's Eve might be fun and plans for the wedding progressed from there. Of course the winter weather could have caused issues but fortunately the January thaw happened the last week of December, which was perfect.

Sara decided to remain in her room until dinner and catch up on some reading while spending the day with Penelope, who was glad to have her home. After unpacking her suitcase and cleaning the litter box, she put on her robe and slippers and got comfortable on the sofa with a good book. This was a perfect day to enjoy the peace and quiet of her apartment. With her wedding anniversary less than a week away her thoughts returned to one of the most challenging times in her married life, the day David confessed his infidelity.

She was devastated and completely blindsided by the news. Her David had been intimate with another woman? Her David had broken the sacred vows of marriage? Her David... No, this wasn't possible. After a brief separation and intense marriage counseling Sara had agreed to reunite with him. It was a very difficult decision, but she felt they were soulmates and his one-night affair was unquestionably poor judgment but shouldn't be grounds for dissolving their marriage.

David was so grateful for being offered a second chance he told her if she decided to leave him permanently he would no longer have a reason for living. She was everything to him and he would never forgive himself for what he did or be able to make up for the grief he had caused her but would spend the rest of his life trying. She had never regretted reuniting with him and they went on to have a long and happy marriage. She closed her eyes and felt a shiver run down her spine, but *what if...*

David travels frequently as a pharmaceutical representative and I have accustomed myself to spending time home alone. When possible I work additional shifts at the hospital to earn more money to put toward the purchase of our first house. We touch base at least once a day but for no more than five minutes because the long-distance phone costs can get quite expensive.

David traveled to Texas for a week in March the year after we celebrated our fifth wedding anniver-

sary for a four-day exposition held by pharmaceutical companies to discuss new products, changes in distribution policies and bottom line—to solicit business. The attendees were wined and dined by the drug companies in an effort to put each one's products at the top of the promotional list. I sometimes went with David, but only when the expos were held in interesting places. This year's show is in a remote area of northern Texas which doesn't appeal to me, so I decide to pass.

David normally calls me in the evening after he returns to his hotel room. On Wednesday evening he calls and we chat a couple of minutes but he seems to be distracted and in a hurry. I didn't think anything of it as it had been a long, busy week and I assume he is tired.

When David returns from that trip he seems different. I can't put my finger on it but something is off. I ask him about it several times the following week and he assures me he's fine and just recuperating from a long week away. I accept his explanation and make a concerted effort to let it go.

When I pick up David's shirts at the cleaners there's is a tag on one of them: "Lipstick stain could not be completely removed from the collar." I read and reread the note in total shock. Why would there be lipstick on my faithful husband's shirt collar? David is at work so I wait until we are eating dinner that night to confront him.

At first he denies it and says the cleaners must be wrong. Then he hangs his head and says he can't carry the guilt another minute. He and another rep from California, Melanie, had been seated next to each other Wednesday evening at dinner. They hit it off and had so much in common. After dinner David returned to his room and called me. After the call he met Melanie in the hotel bar where they talked and had cocktails until the wee hours of Thursday morning. One thing led to another and he awoke to find Melanie next to him in bed.

He is mortified as he had little memory of the prior night. He didn't see her again after she left his room but the damage that was done couldn't be reversed. There is no excuse for what happened. He wants to erase it from his mind and never have that one alcohol-induced indiscretion shatter the love of his life. Keeping the secret is killing him and he is actually glad it's out in the open. After his confession there is dead silence. My David had a one-night fling with a woman in Texas? My soulmate, my life companion, my "until death do us part" husband!

We agree to separate and seek marital counseling. I want so badly to be able to forgive him but my innermost repulsion for what he did won't allow me to. After months of meetings, counseling and efforts to make the marriage work I tell David that I want a divorce.

I truly believed him when he told me it was just this one isolated incident. Had he come home and been man enough to confess what he had done, begging for my forgiveness, I would have still been devastated but I may have found the ability to rebuild our foundation and trust him again one day. His indiscretion coupled with his lying about it is too much for me to forgive. Our marriage is over and although I may never love a man like I loved and continue to love David, I cannot live a life of suspicion and mistrust.

Chapter Sixteen: Connection

fatal procrastination

When Sara rolled over and glanced at the clock, it was three o'clock in the afternoon. She missed lunch and slept soundly for several hours with the vague memory of another time-capsule *what if* moment.

She never regretted her decision to forgive David and move on with their life together but she had to admit, even to herself, that she came awfully close to walking away from the marriage. She had friends on both sides of the marital-indiscretion fence. Some encouraged her to give David another chance because he seemed to be such a nice, sincere, caring man. They told her everyone makes mistakes and although this was a major speed bump on the road to marital bliss; it wasn't worth, to coin a phrase, throwing away the baby with the bath water. Others said that once a man had roaming eyes he could never be trusted again. She would always wonder, when he was away, if he was with another woman.

After weighing the pros and cons, Sara decided that she loved David too much to let this one incident ruin what they had and what was yet to come. She did make it quite clear that any future sexual transgressions would not be forgiven.

Sara wanted to clear her head and felt a nice warm bath would help. As she filled the tub she added her favorite scented bubble bath and inhaled the refreshing floral aroma. A nice soak in the tub always made her feel better and the tub in her apartment had jets that massaged her back as she soaked. It relaxed and exhilarated her at the same time.

As her skin turned prune-like she decided she had soaked long enough and exited the tub as the water drained out slowly. Had it always been this difficult to get out of the tub? For a moment she thought this is what a beached whale must experience. Thank goodness for the handrails.

She rubbed some moisturizing lotion on her arms and legs, trimmed her toe nails, plucked some wild eyebrows, brushed her teeth and applied a bit of blush and lipstick. She felt like a new woman.

She decided to wear the lovely Burberry cashmere classic tartan plaid scarf that Michael had given her for Christmas. It was absolutely beautiful and much too expensive but she loved it. It would become her favorite item of clothing. She wore a red turtleneck sweater and her "old lady" jeans, which meant they fit at her natural waist, not way below it and inches above her private area.

How the younger people are able to wear those fit-below-the-waist low riders remained a mystery to Sara. She bought a pair by mistake once and all day she felt like she needed to pull them up. They went into the charity bin. The clock chimed five and she headed for the elevator to transport her to the dining room level.

The dining room was filling up quickly and only two unoccupied chairs remained at her table. Everyone had returned from their Christmas visits. Deborah immediately recognized the high-end scarf Sara wore and complimented her on it. She feared eating with it on, scared she'd drop food on it and mar its beauty. Although, at her age, she decided not to save any items for later use. Who knew how much later she had left?

Jim provided the table with an upbeat tempo as usual and told the group "I enjoyed spending Christmas here at Parliament Square. The staff made it a holiday to remember. They even offered wine with dinner on Christmas Day, which was quite a treat. One of the residents overindulged and had to be assisted back to her apartment. There's one in every crowd I guess."

Dinner tonight consisted of meatloaf, mashed potatoes and green beans. Sara missed lunch due to her longer than expected nap which resulted in an appetite that allowed her to consume every bit of food on her plate and also take a piece of chocolate cake for dessert. Everyone talked and shared stories of their holiday celebrations with their families. Pam excitedly announced, "I managed to catch a gentleman my age under the mistletoe and steal a Christmas kiss. He was a bit surprised and ran off in search of hand sanitizer and mouth wash. What a spoil sport!"

The group shared stories long after the dishes had been cleared by the waitstaff. Betsy and Jan excused themselves to attend Tuesday night Bingo. The others wished them luck and took a rain check for bingo night another week.

Michele shared a story. "My daughter invited an older gentleman neighbor, who would otherwise be home alone for Christmas dinner, to join us. I think she was trying to play matchmaker but it backfired when our guest tried to catch my daughter under the mistletoe, not me. I can tell you that didn't turn out well. I don't think he'll be invited back again soon."

Deborah excused herself without sharing any personal stories with the group. Joseph seemed especially quiet, but Sara assumed it was because this had been his first Christmas without Theresa. The staff clearly wanted to vacuum the room so the group started to break up. Michele decided to retire for the evening; she had promised her daughter she would check in with her after dinner. Pam also went back to her room to watch a program she taped while away for the weekend. That left Joseph and Sara. They weren't ready to call it a night and decided to sit together in the lobby for a while. They chose a location away from the entrance to the activity room as bingo was in full swing by then.

Joseph surprised Sara as he took her hand in his. He confessed "I missed you while I was away. This Christmas was especially difficult for me. It was wonderful being included for the holidays with my daughter and her family but it just wasn't the same without Theresa. I understand the reality of the situation, but accepting it is still a challenge. I wonder if it will ever get better. Will I ever say Merry Christmas again and truly mean it?"

Sara squeezed Joseph's hand while offering some words of encouragement. "There's no shame in grieving for a loved one, just don't let it interfere with your will to go on. At that point you have to do some thinking and decide if you're grieving for your lost one or if you're grieving for yourself. The spouse left behind often suffers the most, but time can be the ultimate healing force."

They talked about many life events that evening and shared personal moments.

Before they knew it bingo had ended and the participants passed through the lobby on the way to their apartments for the night. Betsy and Jan saw them sitting together and stopped to say goodnight. They were especially animated given that it was after nine. In this establishment, staying up after nine is considered to be wild and crazy behavior. Maybe they drank some caffeinated coffee with their bingo cookies.

Apparently they thought it would be funny to break into a song as they departed the lobby. "Sara and Joseph sitting in a tree, K-I-S-S-I-N-G. First comes love, then comes marriage, then comes baby in a baby carriage!" Sara felt her cheeks flush, but she had to smile a bit as she saw Joseph turn a ghostly shade of pale. Leave it to Betsy and Jan to come up with that song!

Joseph and Sara continued their conversation after the merrily singing duo was out of earshot. "Sara, New Year's Eve is almost here. It would give me great pleasure to take you out for dinner before the party. My daughter has offered to drive us to any restaurant we choose and then bring us back in time for the New Year's Eve party. Would you do me the honor of being my date for the evening?"

Sara was so excited by the invitation that she threw her arms around Joseph and gave him a big hug. "I would love to do that and your daughter is an angel to offer to be our transportation for the evening. It's a date!"

The child-care center closed between the Christmas and New Year holidays, so Sara had both Wednesday and Friday mornings open. She rather missed the routine of being there two mornings a week. It had become part of her weekly schedule.

Cindy solicited residents to assist with the decorations for the New Year's Eve party in the activity room. There would be music, games and dancing. They needed help with the helium balloons, decorations, setting up the tables and chairs and other assorted items. Sara and Joseph volunteered to help on Sunday afternoon for a couple of hours. Once again Jim, by an overwhelming majority was elected the MC for the evening.

Several of the residents contracted this year's strain of the flu and were room bound. Fortunately, no one at Sara's table was affected. Hopefully she would stay healthy to ring in the New Year with Joseph and the others.

This event, because it extended past midnight, was not open to family and friends. Parliament Square didn't want to be responsible for anyone getting in an accident in the early morning of New Year's Day. There would be some beer and wine available, but on a very limited basis.

The newest studies said that drinking small amounts of beer or red wine daily offered health benefits, even outweighing daily exercise. Of course next year those studies could report other findings. In the meantime, Sara planned to have a glass or two of wine to ring in the New Year regardless of whether it was a healthy decision or not.

With the bulk of the preparations completed, Joseph, Sara and the other volunteers were free to return to their rooms or head to the lobby for a visit from the therapy dogs. Sara loved dogs, although she never mentioned that to Penelope. She and David owned an Airedale terrier, Donald, for ten years after they were first married.

David was more of a dog person than Sara, but she had grown to love that little troublemaker. The breed's behavior can be best summed up in one word: enthusiastic. When they lost Donald they decided to defer getting another dog so they could travel without worrying about who would take care of the dog in their absence as David had refused to leave Donald at a dog boarding facility. That's when they became cat people. It was easy enough to have a neighbor or family member stop in to feed and change the litter box when they were away. That, unfortunately, was not the case with a canine companion.

When they got to the lobby, Sue and her therapy dogs were already there. They were such friendly and docile creatures. Sara couldn't imagine her Airedale ever being a therapy dog. He had a lot of energy and his behavior wasn't always exemplary. He loved kids, other dogs and most people. He'd show his affection by putting his paws on your shoulders and licking your face or greeting you with a thorough butt sniffing. That behavior wouldn't work in this environment of fragile and mobility-challenged adults.

Sara and some of the other residents petted and talked to the dogs. They enjoyed the attention and the residents loved it when the dogs visited. Those who lived on the first floor at Parliament Square were allowed to have dogs, but there were guidelines regarding their size and temperament. Also, any resident with a dog must be able to walk it on the outside paths and clean up after it. Sue shared that she would be adopting another dog soon and he would be with her next time.

Sara decided that, since she hoped to stay awake until midnight, she would return to her room for an afternoon siesta before her dinner date with Joseph. When the elevator doors opened she encountered Jean sobbing loudly. "Jean, what's wrong?" she asked.

Jean gasped to regain her composure through the tear shed and said, "Ray has just been taken by ambulance to the hospital. He passed out in the lobby. I'm so worried."

When it happened, Jean rushed to the office and they immediately called 911 to summon an ambulance. He appeared to be responsive as the paramedics put him on the gurney and wheeled him to the ambulance. They asked Jean if she was next of kin and would like to accompany him, but she told them they weren't related.

Jean and Ray were planning to attend the New Year's Eve gala that evening. Sara wasn't sure if Jean was more upset about Ray collapsing or the fact that she wouldn't have a date for the party. Typical Jean behavior, she thought to herself. Or maybe she was being cynical and Jean was really upset about Ray's medical episode. She would give her the benefit of the doubt although she still held a grudge against her over the Halloween situation.

Jean walked toward the office to see if there was any word on Ray's condition. Sara said, "Keep the faith. Hopefully Ray is getting the help he needs and will be back here in no time at all."

Sara continued to her floor. As she exited the elevator a pang of reality struck her with the force of a sledgehammer. Ray's medical emergency could happen to her or Joseph or pretty much any of the other residents at any time. You wake up each morning thankful to be alive but wondering if today is your predetermined expiration date. When a person reaches a certain age, there are no guarantees there will be another tomorrow.

When she was younger, Sara never questioned that tomorrow would be a reality. As she reached middle age there were occasional concerns about health issues, but recovery was expected because she was not "that old." Now in advanced age, disease or health issues could materialize literally overnight and tomorrow is no longer a given. Living a healthy life into your eighties, nineties and even to the century mark is the exception, not the rule. It can be hard to accept at times, but it was the reality of the circle of life. The sand in Sara's hourglass was much fuller at the bottom than it was at the top.

When she entered her apartment Penelope ran to the door to greet her. Sara referred to her as a cat/dog because she was definitely a cat but she sometimes behaved like a dog. She showed her excitement when Sara returned just like a dog would. Some kitties don't even move when their owner arrives, in fact they hide somewhere and often don't surface for hours. That wasn't Penelope. She let Sara know that she enjoyed seeing her every time she returned.

Sara sat on the sofa and encouraged Penelope to join her. "Penelope," she said, "life becomes more fragile with each passing year. We'll all eventually depart this world, but we hope that eventually is later rather than sooner. Don't worry; I plan to take care of you for a long, long time."

Sara wasn't ready to depart just yet. She wanted to see Michael grow his career, prosper (hopefully without the ball and chain) and return from California to be close to her. She wanted to up the ante with Joseph and become a real couple. She wanted a man in her life again. She couldn't believe that her brain thought this way.

All the thinking about age and mortality gave Sara a headache. She wanted to regroup before getting ready for a lovely dinner with Joseph. She took two extra-strength acetaminophen tablets and stretched out on the sofa. Penelope curled up beside her. Soon she became immersed in a dreadfully sad event from her past. Her sister had succumbed to breast cancer at the age of sixty-eight, but *what if...*

I can't remember the last time Barb and I spent the afternoon together. She is always busy with volunteer work and often encourages me to get involved. I tell her that David and I are enjoying our retirement and the cottage by the sea keeps us quite busy. I know that I should somehow help those less fortunate than myself, but after working so many years as a nurse with a difficult schedule, retirement allows me the luxury to start every day with a blank slate. At this point in my life, I don't want a schedule.

We enjoy traveling and experiencing life in other parts of the world. Barb isn't a traveler and after her husband divorced her she funneled all her time and energy into charity work. She is on several committees and boards for organizations that help those without permanent residences, jobs, food and the everyday basics we take for granted. I admire her work and selflessness but I'm not interested in doing the same.

We meet for lunch at a new restaurant in the area that is supposed to have the best sushi in town. I try not to react to Barb's wispy appearance when I first see her but I don't succeed. She must have lost at least twenty pounds since I last saw her. I ask if she's feeling okay and she tells me that she's been rather tired lately, has difficulty sleeping and has an aching pain in her right breast. She is remiss in making her annual mammogram appointment but will call soon.

I'm extremely concerned and after lunch I call and make the appointment for her the following day. She tells me that I'm acting like her mother and

I say that maybe I am but someone has to get the ball rolling.

Barb keeps her appointment and her mammogram shows she has a growth in her right breast. She undergoes further testing and is diagnosed with stage T1a breast cancer which means the cancer has spread into the fatty breast tissue with a tumor the size of a shelled peanut or smaller.

Her physician says that she's incredibly lucky to have caught it in this early stage. Her prognosis is good; she has a lumpectomy and radiation treatments. If she had waited to schedule the mammogram that I demanded she get immediately, her prognosis could have been much different.

As I grow older and less mobile, Barb offers to come live with me at the cottage by the sea so I can stay in my home instead of being moved to a senior living community. I'm so happy she offers to do that. We've never been close as sisters. She is lonely for companionship even with all her charity work and I'm desperate to stay in my cottage. The decision works out well for both of us.

The ringing of the telephone returns Sara to the reality of her apartment and the lingering sadness of her most recent life-choice moment. If only she had insisted her sister schedule that appointment instead of putting it off until months later she might not have succumbed to the disease before she reached the age of seventy. It was an unnecessary tragedy that could have been avoided. Since she lost her sister to the disease, Sara had become an advocate for early detection to anyone and everyone.

Joseph called to remind Sara, "My daughter will be out front to transport us to dinner promptly at seven o'clock. You may want to have an afternoon snack because it won't be the early-bird special dinner menu for us tonight.

Sara responded, "Thanks for the call. I'll have some cheese and crackers to tide me over until dinner. You'll see me in the lobby with bells on promptly at seven." For Sara, this was shaping up to be the best New Year's Eve in years!

Chapter Seventeen: Resolution

destiny

Sara wanted to look her best for the dinner date and ensuing New Year's Eve festivities. Donna did her hair and nails on Saturday afternoon and she went through her entire closet to find a dress that would make her look ten pounds thinner, five or more years younger and like the woman that Joseph couldn't stop admiring. In reality, no such dress exists.

She settled on a calf-length empire-waist peacock-blue dress with a matching fringed shawl. She hadn't worn this since David was alive and she remembered him telling her she looked like royalty in it. She felt strongly that David would approve of her wearing it tonight. In fact, over the past several months, she grew comfortable thinking that David would approve of her friendship with Joseph. He wouldn't expect or want her to stop living and loving in his absence.

Several months before David's accident, after attending a funeral for a friend, Sara and David shared their feelings on how the surviving spouse should handle such a situation. They both agreed that after the grieving process, the remaining spouse should regain some amount of normalcy; romantic involvement should certainly be an option. The living spouse shouldn't be committed to a life of celibacy and loneliness based on honoring the memory of the departed spouse. Doing that would kill the soul of the departed and emotionally destroy the survivor. For the lucky ones, life does go on.

Sara nibbled on some cheese and crackers around 5:00 in an effort to quiet the grumbling noises in her stomach. Since moving to Parliament Square she became accustomed to eating dinner early every evening and her body learned to expect food at that time every day. She didn't want her stomach to embarrass her on the car ride to dinner.

She fed Penelope and started to prepare for the evening. She brushed her teeth and applied a minimal amount of make-up, but tonight she included some mascara to make her thinning eyelashes visible. She fluffed up her hair a bit, put on the blue dress and shawl and posed in front of the full-length mirror, pleased with the final product. Not bad for an old broad, she thought as she gave herself a well-deserved slap on the fanny.

She made a quick call to Michael but he didn't answer so she left him a message wishing him a Happy New Year. It was 6:45 so after giving Penelope a quick hug and executing a couple of runway model poses while winking at her reflection, Sara grabbed her evening clutch and locked the apartment door behind her. Doing that made her laugh out loud.

When the elevator door opened there stood Joseph looking like a page out of *GQ for Seniors*. He wore a tuxedo complete with formal white pleated shirt and black bow tie. His shoes were so shiny that she feared if his foot slipped under the hem of her dress it would reveal her undergarments. He was a sight for sore eyes and Sara was so proud that she had the privilege of being the lady on his arm for the evening.

He said quite loudly, "Sara, you look stunning," without adding *for a woman of your age*. When the elevator stopped at lobby, they headed for the front desk. Since they were leaving the premises, Sara and Joseph were required to sign out with their expected return time.

Cindy complimented them saying, "What a lovely couple you make. You look like you belong together. I hope you have a wonderful dinner together and enjoy the New Year's Eve party later. I'll see you there." As they walked toward the door several of the residents watched them from the sofas. One of them was Jean.

Joseph's daughter, Allison, waited for them in her car. Joseph opened the passenger's door for Sara and she got in. Joseph sat in the back. Allison complimented Sara on how nice she looked and kidded with her dad that he looked extremely dapper for a man in his sixties...*wink, wink*.

Fortunately the weather cooperated and, although it was typical December below-freezing temperatures, there was no ice or snow forecast for tonight or tomorrow. That would be a blessing as so many ring in the New Year and then drive home after drinking. That's bad enough in good weather, but roller-coaster scary in bad weather.

It was a short drive to the restaurant and they arrived a little early for their 7:30 reservation. Not to worry, they could sit at the bar and sip a glass of wine. Allison said, "I'll return around 9:30 to pick you up and drive you back to Parliament Square. If for any reason you aren't ready by then, I will wait until you are. I want to make it quite clear that I'm in no hurry this evening. I'm so happy I'm able to do this for you, Dad, because you've always been there for me." Allison left and they were alone together as a couple.

They found two open barstools, ordered two glasses of wine and soaked in the festive atmosphere. Joseph assisted Sara onto the stool. She loved the feel of his hands around her waist. Her mind kept saying, *He's just a friend* but her heart shouted *He's more than just a friend.*

Celebrating New Year's Eve is like a double-edged sword. It provides an opportunity to look forward to the possibilities of the coming year while lamenting the events of previous years. It's a mixture of endings and beginnings that evokes a blend of emotions ranging from sadness for what had been to hopefulness for what was yet to come. Even when a person's age could be found near the bottom of the life expectancy charts, there should still be positive expectations for what the future might bring.

The hostess announced the Zimmerman table for two was ready. Joseph paid the bartender, helped Sara down from the barstool, and followed her to the table carrying both partially filled glasses of wine. The location of their table was perfect. It was close to the fireplace which was ablaze with warmth and ambiance.

The room was fairly large and quite crowded but table placement and partitioning allowed the diners privacy with a tolerable amount of background noise. They could understand one another without hearing aids or frequent requests for reiteration. Joseph couldn't have selected a better venue for their first dinner date.

The menu was somewhat limited as is often the case on holidays. Sara decided on grilled salmon with a salad and vegetable medley. Joseph ordered the special of the night which was prime rib with a salad and baked potato, butter and sour cream on the side. The rolls were fresh from the oven and served with a side of honey butter. There were no awkward breaks in the conversation as the evening progressed. They talked about many things as they shared dinner, which was as superb as the company.

"Sara, I must confess that I never for a moment thought I would have interest in another woman. Theresa and I were together so many years; we became blended into one person. When I lost her, my world shattered. I didn't want to go on. I seriously thought of taking my own life so that I could be with her again. But I couldn't do that to Allison and my family. Then I met you and the dark clouds started to lift. I felt an immediate attraction to you which at first I struggled to ignore. I thought that feeling affection for another woman would be disrespectful to Theresa's memory so I pushed the feelings away. Then I had a lovely talk with Allison after meeting you. She encouraged me to explore my options as she felt her mother would want me to find happiness in her absence. So, my lovely friend, that is why we are here celebrating one of what I hope will be many New Year's Eves together."

"Thank you so much for sharing that with me," Sarah replied. "I also felt something special from the moment we met. Maybe we're kindred spirits or maybe we have qualities found in our departed spouses. Whatever the case may be, I enjoy our time together and really hope it continues. I don't want to embarrass you but I must say you're one of the most attractive and caring men I have had the pleasure of meeting. Thank you again for dinner and a lovely evening. I too hope this is the first of many evenings we spend together as, I dare say, a couple."

They were just finishing up when Allison arrived. It was a dinner to remember for Sara, she hoped the first of many to come. The ride back to Parliament Square included a cornucopia of dialogue with all three equally contributing. Sara felt so fortunate to have met Joseph and to begin building memories with him. She sensed that Joseph felt the same way. They thanked Allison for the ride and wished her a very Happy New Year. After sharing hugs, they scurried inside as the cold was bitter and the wind was gusty. Sara still disliked the cold Massachusetts winter.

Sara wanted to return to her room to hang up her winter coat, use the bathroom and check on Penelope. Joseph told her that he would meet her in the activity room; he could already hear the music. She hurriedly took care of business and proceeded to the activity room before Jean could possibly corner Joseph to cry on his shoulder about Ray. Probably not a nice thought to have, but she couldn't help herself. She didn't trust Jean and probably never would. Unfortunate but true!

The celebration was in full swing. The music, although loud, was age appropriate, the decorations were glitzy and plentiful and, best of all, there was a great turnout. Sara was quite impressed. Joseph waved to her from the back of the room.

Jean was nowhere in sight. Joseph secured seats at a table away from the music which lowered the volume by several decibels. She was glad to see Betsy and Jan seated at the same table.

They were fully engaged sporting colorful novelty glasses, multiple feather boas and headgear that would make a twelve-point deer jealous. Those two certainly enjoyed life to the fullest without caring one iota about what others thought, which was wonderful and a goal Sara would love to achieve. They complimented Sara on her outfit and said Joseph looked quite formal, like the host of an awards show. They had Sara and Joseph pose for a couple of photos which they took with their cell phones.

Since the number in attendance turned out to be greater than expected, the game choices were somewhat limited. There had been some bingo earlier in the evening but that was over before Sara and Joseph arrived. Cindy was organizing a game of musical chairs in the middle of the room while others sat at tables chatting and sipping wine from plastic glasses.

A professional DJ played the music, a combination of classics from the forties, fifties and sixties which fit this crowd perfectly. There were opportunities to dance the stroll, the jitterbug, the twist and, of course, the nice slow dances.

Although these vintage partygoers weren't as flexible and nimble as they used to be, they still enjoyed dancing. Those who didn't or couldn't participate on the dance floor sat on the sidelines clapping and cheering for those who did. Some in wheelchairs tapped their feet to the beat. In our mind's eye we still see ourselves dancing like we did in our prime. We still feel the beat but have lost the ability to respond to it.

Sara and Joseph mostly danced to the slower songs but they couldn't resist shaking their seasoned booties to the twist. A bit winded, they returned to the table and sat out several dances while they caught their breath.

The time passed quickly. Jim sprinkled jokes between sets. He announced that he had a knock-knock joke. The crowd groaned. Jim said, "Knock Knock."

The crowd responded in unison, "Who's there?"

"Mary and Abby."

"Mary and Abby who?"

"Mary Christmas and a Abby New Year!" Audible groans.

Jim assured everyone that he had only one final joke before he signed off for the evening. He said, "Instead of the John, I call my bathroom the Jim. That way it sounds better when I say I go to the Jim first thing every morning!" Unfortunately, there were no rotten tomatoes to throw so instead the crowd all blew their horns and shook their noisemakers to let Jim know how much they liked or disliked—it was hard to tell the difference—his jokes.

The last song was Paul Anka's "You Are My Destiny" which had the perfect tempo for a close, slow dance. Sara wondered if Joseph could be her destiny.

Cindy and her assistants handed out noise makers and horns in preparation for midnight. Sara hadn't been with a man on New Year's Eve for five years since she shared her last New Year's Eve kiss with David the month before he died. She was hoping that Joseph planned to change that.

The crowd grew loud as they watched the broadcast from Times Square on the big-screen TV. The ball started to descend at exactly 11:59 and the crowd started to count down the seconds until January 1st.

Sara made sure that she was next to Joseph so they could usher in the New Year with a much-anticipated kiss. The noisemakers and horns filled the room with deafening noise and Joseph turned to Sara, wished her a Happy New Year and ever so softly pressed his lips to hers. She melted into his arms and enjoyed the moment as much or more as her very first kiss with Alan West on the bleachers during a high school football game in seventh grade.

"Auld Lang Syne" began to play and Sara was overcome with emotion. She didn't know if she cried because she missed all the good years she had with David or because she was grateful to have Joseph in her life. She dabbed her eyes, blew her noisemaker and wished Joseph a Happy New Year. What a wonderful way to begin another year!

The party concluded soon after midnight. Most residents weren't night owls although many got up during the night for bathroom breaks or because they nodded off in front of the television at 8:30 PM and just couldn't sleep any longer.

Studies show that people of advanced years don't need as much sleep as their younger counterparts; however, adding up daily naps, early bedtimes and the semi-comatose hours spent each day in front of the television could nullify those studies.

After exchanging New Year wishes, hugs and kisses everyone headed to their apartments for the night. Joseph whispered to Sara that he had a wonderful evening and hoped they could spend many more New Year Eves together. She thanked him for sharing the best night she could remember in many years. He pecked her on the cheek and bade her pleasant dreams. After tonight, what other kind of dreams could there be?

Once in bed Sara hugged one pillow tightly and said her nightly prayers, asking that the feelings she shared this evening for Joseph were reciprocated. She never thought that she would feel this way about a man again and now that she did, she never wanted the feeling to end. No matter what your age when love finds you, don't ever say you are too old to accept it. Love knows no boundaries. She blissfully surrendered to slumber, content in the knowledge that destiny brought she and Joseph together. Destiny was indeed the mistress of romance.

When she was younger she used to question destiny; her logical way of thinking didn't support it, but then something happened when she and David were leaving for a vacation to Egypt. Many of her friends told her they truly believed destiny played a major role in this event.

Sara's perpetual tardiness actually saved their lives when they missed boarding Egypt Air Flight 990 after midnight on Halloween in 1999 at John F. Kennedy International Airport. Sara could never forget how frustrated and upset David was with her that day. He later apologized and thanked her for unknowingly saving their lives, but *what if* they had been on time that fateful October day?

"Sara, I'm not going to remind you again what time it is. We have a five-hour drive ahead of us. I told you we should have driven there yesterday and stayed in a hotel.

"We still have plenty of time to get there," Sara replied. David gets so upset with my lackadaisical attitude when it comes to schedules and timeliness. A couple of minutes one way or the other isn't going to make a difference.

We've been planning our trip to Egypt for months. We love traveling to foreign countries and can't wait to visit the Great Pyramids, the Sphinx, the Abu Simbel temples, the Karnak Temple Complex, the Valley of Kings near Luxor and the sights in Cairo. We decide not to travel with a group. Although we're in our sixties, we're both still quite active and have no mobility issues. The trip will last two weeks and we plan to spend every day exploring the history and culture of Egypt.

The weather is good as we leave Massachusetts and head to JFK in New York. All goes well for the first three hours. Then we see red brake lights ahead, miles and miles of them. Traffic comes to a standstill.

Fortunately, we are routed around the accident and we arrive at the airport in plenty of time to check in and get ready to board our flight, Egypt Air Flight 990, a direct flight to Cairo.

We board the plane shortly after 12:30 AM and find our seats. The flight, which originated in Los Angeles, has many seats already occupied, with passengers sleeping or resting in their seats as we settle in for the trip.

Takeoff is uneventful, but shortly into the flight every passenger's worst nightmare comes to fruition. First, a rapid nose dive and everything in the cabin becomes weightless. Then the plane enters a steep climb and everyone is thrust hard back into their seats. Then quiet and darkness as the engines stop.

The plane crashes nose-first into the Atlantic at 1:52 AM killing all passengers and crew aboard the flight, 217 fatalities. David and I are killed on impact.

Sara awoke with her heart pounding and her nightgown wet with perspiration. That moment was so frightening even after the almost twenty years since it happened. At the time, Sara felt that she and David were spared because their expiration dates didn't match that fateful day in October, but what about those who died in the crash? Their dates couldn't all have matched that of the relief first officer who piloted the aircraft. The investigation indicated that he appeared to have been on a suicide mission, thus superseding the expiration date theory as he tied his fate to the fates of all the passengers and crew members by his actions.

Sara and David dodged what would have been a fatal bullet and, although distraught over the tragedy, they forged ahead and caught a flight the very next day.

Chapter Eighteen:
Reflection

vice versa

Each new calendar year brings with it the possibility to build new friendships, the opportunity to strengthen existing relationships, the ability to encounter new experiences and the expectation of new memories that will, with any luck, last a lifetime.

January is a month filled with resolutions for the coming year (often not accomplished), new gym memberships (often not utilized) and hopefulness for a year of good health, wealth and happiness (often not achieved). As we age we hope it's not the year that will be etched into our headstones.

Baby New Year wears a diaper, top hat and sash with the new year printed on it while Father Time is an old bearded man dressed in a long robe and sash with the previous year printed on it, carrying an hourglass and scythe.

These symbols illustrate the birth of the new year, full of promise, and the death of the old year, drained of life. Much like the cycle of life, with youthfulness often taken for granted and greatly underappreciated, until in the blink of an eye it vanishes and is replaced with the winter of life.

Sara enthusiastically returned to the daycare center on Wednesday morning. She missed spending time with the children over the Christmas break. It was her turn to read the morning story and Sara chose *The Little Engine That Could*. It had always been one of her favorites and she fondly remembered reading it to Michael when he was young.

She loved the story of the little train succeeding through strong belief and hard work, values children are never too young to learn. Some of the newer children's books are more boldly and colorfully illustrated and include more humor but they don't have messages like this one does. The children probably won't realize that, but Sara will.

She read the book to the children and asked them to say the words "I think I can, I think I can, I think I can" along with her as the engine climbed the hill pulling a long line of freight cars. Then when the engine made it over the top, she asked the children to say "I thought I could, I thought I could" with her. They enjoyed the story and helping her tell it. They were too young to truly understand the moral but not too young to understand the little engine's success.

Sara and Joseph had chatted at the dinner table with their dining companions since New Year's Eve but they hadn't talked in private since then. Sara reflected on that evening's events. She really enjoyed being with Joseph for dinner, dancing together and the wonderful New Year's Eve kiss.

Could those be the building blocks of a permanent romantic relationship? Dare she even think those thoughts at her age? Never in her wildest dreams could she have imagined feeling the way she felt when she was with Joseph. She wondered if this year would bring them closer together and perhaps just possibly allow them to begin a new chapter together in their eighty-plus-year book of life.

One evening, after dinner, Joseph asked Sara if she would join him in his apartment as he had something to discuss with her that was best done in private. Sara's heart fluttered and for a moment she felt like a giddy schoolgirl. She told herself to get a grip, he may simply want to discuss a new book he was reading, review a current event or talk about the upcoming Valentine's Day party. She was very hopeful that he would ask her to be his date for the evening.

When they reached his apartment, they went inside and sat together on the sofa. Joseph nervously fluffed a couple of the throw pillows and repositioned the candy dishes on the coffee table until they were in perfect alignment. Sara sensed Joseph was uncomfortable and she became scared that he was about to deliver bad news. She braced herself for the worst. Instead, Joseph said, "I must confess that I still deeply miss Theresa. Last night she came to me in a dream telling me to find happiness and move on with my life. She doesn't want me to grieve her loss anymore and be alone. It was so real. I awoke in a sweat with my heart racing. I immediately got up and wrote it all down so I wouldn't forget it. I don't believe in ghosts or spirits but this almost made me a believer."

Wow, that was not what Sara expected. Actually, she really didn't know what she expected. Worst-case scenario, Joseph would tell her that he didn't want their relationship to continue or to grow. Best-case scenario, Joseph would confess his undying love to her. This was not exactly either worst or best case, but it was certainly closer to best than to worst.

Thoughts swirled around in her head. *Was she really ready to make a permanent commitment to another man? What would life be like living with a man again? Someone other than Penelope would see her in her birthday suit, which was in desperate need of a good pressing.* Living with another person after being alone for many years can be a difficult adjustment. People become set in their ways, especially as they get older. Although they say love is blind that doesn't pertain to wet towels on the bathroom floor, open toilet seats and dirty dishes in the sink.

Maybe a nice friendship with benefits (though limited as octogenarians) would be better than marriage, commitment and permanently living together. But she was putting the cart before the horse. That was a discussion best left for another day.

Joseph and Sara shared some decaffeinated coffee (caffeine was her kryptonite after noon), delicious butter cookies and watched the evening game shows together in his apartment. It was nice having some private time together away from the other residents. Sara thought this might be the next step in strengthening their relationship.

They competed to see who could answer the questions and puzzles first and laughed out loud at a couple of the sitcoms that followed. It certainly was an enjoyable evening. Around ten o'clock Sara said "I must be going. Penelope will be getting lonely. Thank you so much for your hospitality and being comfortable enough to share your personal feelings with me. I really enjoy the time we spend together."

As she was leaving Joseph gave her a quick hug and a peck on the cheek. "Thank you for being such a good listener and sharing the evening with this antique. I also enjoy the private time we share."

Several weeks passed after that evening together with Sara and Joseph not having any one-on-one time. They attended some of the same group activities which included a bowling night, a charades night and several exercise classes. Sara enjoyed her Wednesday and Friday mornings volunteering in the daycare center while Joseph spent some time in the on-site woodshop, building some birdhouses to put out in the spring. They seemed to be fitting into the daily routine at Parliament Square and adjusting to their newfound home.

Sara saw Jean in the lobby one morning and asked, "How is Ray doing? I haven't seen him around since his emergency."

Jean replied, "He had a mild heart attack but is doing well. His daughter insists that he stay with her while he recovers. Right now I'm unsure when or if he'll be back. How are you and Joseph doing? People are talking about you two being a couple. I don't always believe what I hear; some of these people are out of touch with reality."

Sara simply replied, "Joseph is doing quite well." This provided Sara the perfect opportunity to tell Jean about their New Year's Eve kiss, the lovely flowers with the note, and the evenings spent together, but she didn't really like Jean or want to share personal information with her. Better to keep her guessing. "Hopefully Ray will recover quickly and return back here soon." Sara feared that Jean would reactivate her quest for Joseph's affections and forget all about Ray. As the saying goes, *Out of sight, out of mind.* Sara didn't trust Jean.

One Thursday evening Sara sat in the lobby watching a new clean layer of snow cover the grey, dirty piles left behind from the previous storm when Joseph appeared out of nowhere and sat next to her. He said, "I just got off the telephone with my daughter. She invited me to come spend the weekend while the boys are away on a ski trip. It'll just be Allison and her husband, William. She also said they'd love it if you could come along. The plan is to make dinner reservations at their favorite restaurant for Saturday night and we'll all attend church together on Sunday morning before returning to Parliament Square. I told Allison that I'd discuss it with you and let her know. What do you think?"

"Joseph, that is a splendid idea and I'd love to go. With Michael in California I don't have many opportunities to get away from here and experience the outside world. Please let Allison know that I enthusiastically accept her generous invitation for a weekend visit. It'll give me a chance to spend some time with her and get the inside scoop on her father. I'm so excited!"

"Sara, I am going to return to my room right now and tell her that you'll be spending the weekend with us. Have a good evening and pleasant dreams." Before he departed, he squeezed Sara's hand and gave her a quick kiss on the cheek.

Sara no longer experienced the alternate life-choice what if moments as frequently as she had when she moved to Parliament Square. She wondered if that meant she was accepting her new surroundings. Maybe the stress and anxiety of her relocation were the causes of those moments.

As she relaxed in her room reflecting on some of the previous through-the-looking-glass moments, she was transported yet one more time...

I was sitting in a church decorated with beautiful flowers as the wedding march started to play.

Those seated in the pews stood and turned to see the bride walking down the aisle. The bride was Jean.

Betsy and Jan are so excited to be bridesmaids. Their dresses resembled large flowers with poufy sleeves literally the size of beach balls, the color a blend of banana yellow and kiwi green with strawberry highlights. Matching Carmen Miranda fruit hats were all they needed to complete the ensemble.

It was the first wedding in a long time for the residents of Parliament Square. We attended many, many more funerals than weddings. Joseph looked nervous standing at the front of the church with Jim and Ray at his side. Jean smiled triumphantly as she walked down the aisle.

I guess Jean's purchase of the Little Red Riding Hood costume had started this whole relationship. How ironic that I selected the exact costume but I wasn't the one walking down the aisle to begin a life with Joseph.

Since the night of the Halloween party Jean had relentlessly pursued Joseph. She convinced him that he was lonely since losing Theresa, he needed a new woman in his life and she wanted to be that woman. Joseph was too polite, or maybe too tired, sad and weak, to disagree and so the dice had been rolled. The minister pronounced them Mr. and Mrs. Joseph Zimmerman and told Joseph he could kiss the bride. I felt like someone had punched me in the stomach.

That brief what-could-have-been moment was more like a nightmare. Sara felt drained but she was relieved to realize it wasn't reality. If Joseph had been a weaker man he could have succumbed to Jean's affections and been swept into a relationship and possible marriage out of convenience and complacency. Jean could have been a comfortable companion for him in his twilight years after the loss of Theresa. Fortunately, he realized Jean wasn't for him.

At any age, a marriage without love is like lyrics without music, spaghetti without meatballs, yin without yang. Reviewing that brief moment seeing Jean and Joseph together made Sara empathize a bit with Jean. Seeing her and Joseph together must be a difficult pill for Jean to swallow. Hopefully Ray's recovery and return would happen and happen soon.

Saturday was ushered in with bright sunshine and a clear blue sky. No winter storms on the horizon to postpone the weekend trip to see Allison and her husband. Sara anticipated the trip with mixed emotions. She was honored that both Allison and Joseph wanted her to spend the weekend with them but she was nervous about what to expect. She never met Joseph's son-in-law, William, and had only spent a limited amount of time with Allison.

She hoped there would not be awkward and uncomfortable breaks in the conversation or dozens of pictures of Theresa displayed throughout the house. Certainly Allison had every right to display pictures of her parents in her home and Sara had no intention of competing with the memory of Allison's mother and Joseph's wife.

Family photos are cherished reminders of times spent together after the people in the pictures are no longer with us. They bring back memories, reminding us of the happiness of the past followed by a deep emptiness of what was no more. It was a fine line with muted boundaries and jagged edges.

Sara packed and repacked her clothing choices for the weekend several times. She didn't want to look like Granny on *The Beverly Hillbillies* but she also didn't want to look like an older person trying to look younger by dressing in a young person's clothing. She went with dark colors, nothing form-fitting and no skirts. The Burberry scarf that Michael gave her for Christmas was included. She planned to wear that when they went out to dinner on Saturday evening. She felt as nervous as Nellie on a bad day!

Allison and William's house was lovely. William had an athletic build with a full head of hair and dark eyebrows that contrasted sharply with his almost silver hair. He was quite gracious but she sensed an underlying tension with Joseph. He asked Sara to please call him Bill.

Joseph gave Sara a tour after which they put their bags in two of the guest rooms. It was a large house with five bedrooms, four full baths, a gourmet kitchen and lots of amenities. Allison mentioned that once the boys graduated from college and found full-time employment, she hoped to downsize. Sara did notice some pictures of Joseph and Theresa scattered throughout the house but there weren't enough to make her feel uncomfortable.

Sara commented on the beautiful grand piano in the living room and Allison begged Joseph to play something for them. Sara didn't realize that Joseph was a pianist but there were probably many things that she didn't know about this man. Maybe there were dark, mysterious secrets to be unveiled, or maybe there were skills and talents hidden below the surface yet to be uncovered.

Joseph reluctantly played several songs from memory, which was quite impressive. Sara asked if by any chance he knew the song *Moments to Remember* made famous in the 50's by the Four Lads. Joseph turned a ghostly pale upon hearing the request. That song had been one of Theresa's favorites and he knew it very well. He played the song and Sara sang the lyrics silently in her head...

Though summer turns to winter
And the present disappears

The laughter we were glad to share
Will echo through the years

The words took Sara and Joseph for a stroll down memory lane. This was the song Sara asked to be played at her wedding reception as she danced with her father. Small world!

Sara took piano lessons and learned how to play when she was growing up but Barb, her younger sister, had been born with extraordinary musical talent and soon became the accomplished musician in the family. Competing with her was both futile and frustrating. Sara still enjoyed sitting at her piano and playing a bit but her ability was nowhere close to Joseph's.

While Joseph and William watched sports Sara and Allison decided to visit the mall for winter specials. Sara really needed a new purse, so finding one was the goal for the trip. On the ride to the mall, Allison shared some family history.

"My parents met in college and got married soon after graduation. They both had been business majors and decided to build a family business together instead of going into sales or taking desk jobs crunching numbers or marketing someone else's products. They explored their options and although they had no knowledge or experience in the restaurant business, they decided to open a family restaurant.

"It was years of long hours and hard work and they came close to filing bankruptcy twice. The first five years were the hardest but after that the business flourished and the restaurant became a popular local landmark. Ever since I can remember I was at the restaurant more than I was at home. I grew up there and as soon as I was old enough I helped my parents with the business, although I knew it wasn't what I wanted to do with my life."

Sara found all of this immensely interesting. More information she didn't know about Joseph. Allison went on to say,

"My father's investments in the stock market using the profits from the business had, over time, grown substantially. They made my parents millionaires several times over. Even with that much wealth, they refused to retire early and sell the restaurant. It was too much a part of them.

"When they were in their seventies I finally convinced them to sell the restaurant and enjoy their retirement. They've done just that. They traveled extensively for almost a decade. Then my mother's health forced them to stay home and her passing left my father alone for the first time since his college days.

"He didn't know how to function without her and the first couple of months I thought he was going to die of a broken heart. He lived alone for a while but it was obvious that he wasn't happy living in the house. He fell into a deep depression and stopped taking care of the house and himself. It was getting out of control. He wouldn't move in with me. He said he didn't want to be a burden. That's when I decided to move him to Parliament Square.

"It was difficult for everyone but as the months passed I thought he was beginning to adjust to life there. Then one day he told me that he made a new friend. He told me that he felt an immediate connection with her and, for the first time since moving there, he didn't feel alone."

Wow, that was a lot for Sara to process. She hadn't known that Joseph was a successful restaurant owner or that he was quite a wealthy man. She knew that Parliament Square was not inexpensive, which had bothered her because she wasn't a wealthy woman, but Michael had convinced her that she could afford to live there after the sale of her cottage and she believed him. She did worry at times about what would happen when her money ran out, but somewhere in the reams of paperwork that she had signed before moving in, all that had been addressed and documented.

By the time they got to the mall Sara had almost forgotten what she wanted to buy. They walked slowly through the shops, protected from the cold winter outside. They shared a delicious cinnamon roll and coffee together at the food court and did some people watching.

They window shopped and laughed about the provocative fashion trends of the younger generation. They found the perfect purse for Sara. It was roomy with lots of zippered compartments, a neutral color, a popular brand name and best of all, it was on sale at forty percent off. The clerk rang up the sale and Sara told Allison, "I'm ready to call it a day. My comfortable walking shoes aren't living up to their description."

The ride back to the house was short and Sara thanked Allison for an enjoyable afternoon. Allison said, "I had a wonderful time talking and sharing time with you. I hope we can do this again soon."

They arrived back at the house in time for Sara to take a quick nap before getting ready for their Saturday night dinner. Joseph had fallen asleep on the sofa watching golf on television. How anyone watched that for more than ten minutes and remained awake Sara would never understand.

She quietly went up to her room, kicked off her not-so-comfortable walking shoes, reflected on the day's activities and fell into a much needed slumber. She almost expected a what if moment, but she fell asleep peacefully, undisturbed by dreams of what might have been.

Chapter Nineteen: Conclusion

the announcement

When Sara rolled over and saw the clock she couldn't believe her eyes. Was she inside another moment in time? Where was she? It was almost six o'clock in the evening. She dozed off for nearly two hours. She remembered that she was in a bedroom at Allison's house and decided to take a catnap after they returned from shopping.

Why hadn't anyone awakened her for dinner? Had they left without her? Then there was a soft tap on the door. It was Allison. "The reservation isn't until 7:00, so there's still plenty of time for you to get ready. I'm so glad that you could take a rest and recharge. We'll be leaving at 6:45 for dinner. Please join us in the living room when you're ready."

Sara decided to empty her old purse and transfer the contents to the new one she bought that day. It would go nicely with the outfit she packed to wear to dinner. While she brushed her teeth, refreshed her blush and lipstick and dressed, her mind reviewed what Allison had shared with her during their car ride.

Joseph had retired from being the co-owner of a popular restaurant in the area and apparently is quite wealthy. There was still so much to learn about the quiet handsome gentleman to whom she was so attracted. She was glad that Allison had invited her to spend the weekend. Or could it have been Joseph's idea? Did he want to take their friendship to another level? Maybe Sara was overthinking things. Be patient and let nature take its course, she thought as she walked to the living room.

Allison offered her a glass of wine and she cordially accepted. She told herself she drank wine purely for the health benefits, but the truth of the matter was she really enjoyed a glass of wine now and then.

The evening news was on television in the background. She seldom watched it anymore as it was just too depressing.

What was this world coming to with all the crime and violence? Give her the "good old days" anytime.

Joseph looked so handsome in his navy-blue blazer which accented the blue of his eyes. William talked on his phone with one of the boys discussing their ski weekend. The trip was going well with stellar weather conditions, including new powder which Sara remembered from her skiing days could make the skier feel like he or she was literally floating. She missed those days, but at her age she chose not to risk the possibility of any broken bones or other injuries. Healing just took too darn long if it was even possible.

The ride was short, less than ten minutes. Sara and Joseph sat in the back listening to jazz that was crisply broadcast via top-of-the-line speakers. They were going to the restaurant that had been owned by Joseph and his wife. The new owner had changed the name and made extensive renovations, but it was still the same location.

Sara thought that this must be bittersweet for Joseph. Although it's completely understandable that new owners modify real estate, personalizing it to their style, it can be difficult for the original owner to accept the changes in a place that is so anchored to years of personal history.

Sara never wanted to return to her cottage by the sea to see what transformations the new owners may have made. The seller had no claim to a property after it was sold, but modifications made by new owners could erase years of memories.

Arriving right on time, they were immediately seated at a table located close to a large floor-to-ceiling fireplace adorned with ornate mosaic tilework and elaborate wooden accents. It was the focal point of the large dining room. This was definitely an upscale establishment.

The waitstaff all wore white shirts or blouses with black trousers or slacks. All the males were clean-shaven with none sporting the new hair sensation for men, the man bun. All the females had either short hair or longer hair secured in a pony-tail or upsweep.

Sara wondered for a moment what life would be like as a young person today. Everything was so hurried. Electronics were an integral part of life and a real game changer. Each generation reflects back on what things were like for them when they were young. Given the chance, how many would choose to grow up in today's world instead of the world of their memories? Times were so much simpler and less complicated when Sara was young.

The menu selections were quite extensive. Allison said on the ride over that she loved their grilled salmon topped with mango chutney, although she went on to say that they had never been disappointed with anything they'd had.

Joseph shared, "The specialty of the restaurant when it was under our management was the filet mignon. It was first marinated using a secret family recipe, the *Three S*—sweet, salty, and spicy—marinate. The steak was seared to darken the surface, while retaining the juices, and then placed in a hot oven to finish cooking to the desired wellness. Just talking about it makes my mouth to water."

Their waiter, Matthew, recited all the evening's specials. How do people remember all that information, Sara wondered? It must have something to do with younger, more abundant brain cells.

They placed their orders and munched on the crusty rolls until their salads arrived. Dinner conversation was pleasant but generic. Saying the food was excellent was an understatement. This was probably the best meal Sara had eaten in a long, long time. They all passed on dessert. Allison and William ordered after-dinner drinks while Joseph and Sara opted for a cup of decaf.

When Matthew brought the check William almost grabbed it out of his hand. "This is my treat even though

Joseph offered several times to cover the damages. Joseph, you can pay the next time." Again, Sara sensed tension.

The remainder of the weekend was delightful. Allison baked homemade cinnamon rolls for breakfast. On Sunday they attended a small non-denominational church close to home. The congregation welcomed them like they were long-lost friends. It was almost like a family had gathered together on Sunday morning to sing, pray and listen to the sermon. Sara liked that and felt guilty for not attending services since moving to Parliament Square even though transportation to several churches was available.

She was not a consistent churchgoer when she lived in her cottage. Religion was important to her but she often felt more comfortable reading devotional material alone rather than in an organized setting. It was a personal choice but she was glad to experience the worship service that Sunday with Allison and Joseph. William had stayed home using the excuse that he would clean up the breakfast dishes while they were gone. Sara sensed that attending church wasn't an event William relished.

Afterward they stopped on the way back to Parliament Square to share a light lunch together. Sara told Allison, "I had a wonderful weekend and thank you so much for your warm hospitality."

Alison replied, "So glad you enjoyed our dinner out together. That venue would be a perfect location for any future celebrations the folks at Parliament Square plan. I'm counting the days until the Valentine's Day dance. This is all so exciting." To Sara, that almost sounded like the weekend visit was planned to set the stage for an upcoming event. Before she could ask any questions Joseph's eyes darted to Allison and he quickly changed the subject. Sara wondered what that was all about.

Back at Parliament Square, Sara and Joseph hugged Allison, said their farewells and carried their overnight bags into the lobby. Sara said, "I want to visit with Michele a bit since we haven't been able to spend much time together. I feel a little guilty about that. The weekend was wonderful and I'm so thankful that I could spend time with Allison and William. I felt just like one of the family. You're so lucky to have a wonderful daughter who lives so close to you. You should be very thankful."

Once inside her apartment, and after briefly reuniting with Penelope, Sara called Michele to invite her over for tea and "girl talk." Michele told Sara she would see her in thirty minutes.

Sara understood that Michele, like most who moved to Parliament Square, would have an adjustment period. The transition for some was seamless while for others it was as rough as the jagged edges of a broken bottle. Sara hoped that Michele was becoming comfortable with her new surroundings and daily routine.

Penelope jumped down from the chair when she heard the knock on the door. Sara hugged Michele and welcomed her inside. It was so good having a friend here now that she could confide in and with whom she could share personal stories. She wanted someone to talk to about Joseph.

She missed Michael and didn't want their weekly chats consumed by talk about herself. She wanted to know how he was doing with his new job, his new apartment and, most of all, how Marcy was adjusting (or not) to her new surroundings.

Over tea and cookies, Sara and Michele shared feelings, personal news and friendship. Sara said, "There's going to be an opening at the childcare center Wednesday and Friday mornings. You should sign up. Just think of all the things it'll give us to talk about! I'm so glad that you moved here.

If there's anything I can do to help you adjust, please let me know. I had a difficult time for a while. It's certainly a change in lifestyle and, at our age, change can be hard to accept, but I've made new friends and now I have an old friend to make new memories with."

Michele responded enthusiastically. "I'll sign up tomorrow morning first thing. I love children. I am a bit bored with my everyday routine even though I tried several group activities over the past few weeks. Our apartments say 'independent senior living,' but it doesn't always feel that way." Sara said that she couldn't agree more.

That evening at dinner all the chairs were occupied. Sara sat between Michele and Joseph. Betsy and Jan shared stories about their annual college alumni weekend. They reminisced about the four years they lived together at college and the walk down memory lane they took each year when they attended the alumni event. It was sad to discover that some classmates had departed since last year's event, or to hear of those who couldn't attend because of health issues. It was simply a matter of time until there was no one left from the class of 1957, but until then Jan and Betsy planned to attend every year that they were physically able. Good for them, Sara thought.

This reminded Jim of a joke (really, what didn't remind him of a joke?). He said, "When I die, I want to go peacefully, the way my uncle did, in his sleep. Not screaming like the passengers in his car!" Everyone laughed, but Sara really did hope to go peacefully. Unfortunately, in the overall scheme of our future and eventual demise, we have little if any input.

There are so many who experience incredible pain and suffering for extended periods before succumbing to an illness. One of the most frightening questions to think about when approaching your statistical expiration date: What will be listed on your death certificate as cause of death? Everyone if given the choice, would prefer a quick, painless end but that, unfortunately, is decided by a much higher power.

After dinner Joseph and Sara joined Jan and Betsy in the activity room for bingo night. Sara had attended several times, but this was the first time for Joseph. They chatted a little before the event got started. Joseph asked, "Sara, will you be my date for the St. Valentine's dance?"

Sara accepted immediately and said, "I can't wait to dance together again like we did on New Year's Eve. This time I'll try to let you lead. It's a date!"

Celeste and her band of refreshment-table renegades entered the activity room and reserved their seats. Jan and Betsy made some comments under their breath and grabbed two seats at the same table, close to the refreshment table.

Jan wore her lucky hat which could best be described as the illegitimate child of a relationship between a Mardi Gras headpiece and a Mummer's costume. Betsy carried a keychain with a lucky rabbit's foot (was there even a rabbit with a foot that big?) and a four-leaf clover. Sara and Joseph sat further back in the room and took their chances on refreshment availability after the last game was called. These ladies took their bingo night seriously.

Jean joined Joseph and Sara. She said that Ray was doing well and expected to be back at Parliament Square in time for the Valentine's Day party. Although Sara didn't trust Jean, she felt a bit sorry for her. She tried her best to be courteous and act concerned about Jean's anxiety issues which Jean had no difficulty sharing in great detail. She still wouldn't turn her back on Jean, fearing she'd pounce on any opportunity to get closer to Joseph. Little did Jean know that Joseph didn't welcome her interest.

The numbers for the first game were announced and the evening's activities were under way. Although Sara enjoyed attending since Joseph was with her, bingo wasn't high on her list of fun things to do. It filled the long dark winter evening with socializing, refreshments and prizes, but she would rather be with Joseph watching the game shows and sharing some tea and cookies.

With the Valentine's Day party fast approaching, Sara took the bus with Michele one afternoon to the mall to shop for something new to wear. She really didn't need a new outfit but she wanted one anyway. The trendy storefronts targeting the younger buyers were plentiful, but their styles certainly didn't run parallel to Sara's tastes. Then there were the larger department stores that carried clothing for customers ranging from newborn to casket-ready.

Sara and Michele tried on several outfits in three stores and critiqued each other's choices. Some selections were vetoed because they made them look heavy or they emphasized the wrong body parts, or the color didn't compliment their skin tone. There were more thumbs down than thumbs up. Eventually, Sara decided on a stunning red sweater, perfect for Valentine's Day, with a mock-turtle neck which would hide some of her wrinkles without making her look like a turtle. It had three-quarter-length sleeves and a soft-as-a-baby's-behind texture that felt like cashmere but was much less expensive. Sara told Michele that she'd pass on new pants because she had so many already. The red color would be perfect for Valentine's Day.

Michele passed on any new clothing because she hadn't been invited to the dance and wasn't sure if she was going. Although an escort certainly wasn't necessary, it made the event more exciting for those who had one.

Michele, being a woman of color, was in the minority at Parliament Square where over ninety percent of the residents were white. She was all right with that because the neighborhood she moved from had about the same ethnic ratio.

She had long ago learned to accept stares from others. Her husband, who predeceased her, was a white man. After their marriage, they experienced many years of being pointed at and whispered about, but they weathered the storm and, as the years passed, so did much of the racial prejudice. There was a much greater acceptance of interracial couples since their marriage in 1965, but even in the twenty-first century much recognition and acceptance was still needed.

Sara and Michele had a wonderful shopping trip and really enjoyed being able to spend some one-on-one time away from the boundaries of Parliament Square. They told their dining companions about their day together that evening. Betsy and Jan gave them a thumbs-up while Jim and Joseph immediately returned to talking about the upcoming March Madness. Pam was in her own little they-know-me-here world and Deborah was her usual introverted self. They were quite a potpourri of individuals. Fortunately, politics and religion were rarely discussed.

Sara was finally comfortable with her new home and neighbors. She missed her cottage by the sea less and embraced life at Parliament Square more. She discussed this with Michael during their most recent long-distance conversation, but she could tell that he was distracted. He said, "I have serious concerns that Marcy and I may not be well suited for each other. My job is going great and I love the California weather but Marcy can be such a Debbie Downer (Michael had to explain what that meant), always raining on my parade.

"We've been going to marriage counseling. Please don't worry about me; I'll be fine whether Marcy and I work our issues out or not. I'm so glad that you're adjusting and you have Michele and Joseph in your life to fill the void left when I kind of abandoned you. Before I move back to Massachusetts you have to come visit me. I want to show you the sights and share my new world with you."

Sara said, "Maybe, if I could take the train, that might just work."

The morning of the Valentine's Day party Sara enjoyed breakfast in the dining room but Joseph wasn't there. She would check on him after breakfast, she thought. Maybe he decided to sleep late or maybe he attended one of the early-morning exercise classes.

Sara especially liked Cynthia, who had the energy level of the "Energizer Bunny" after drinking a double espresso. She really got the group off their senior citizen derrieres as her level of enthusiasm was contagious. She advised those in the class to work within their comfort zone while at the same time encouraging them to challenge themselves to do more. She was quite entertaining and her classes were full most days.

Sara called Joseph after she finished her breakfast. He answered on the third ring and told Sara that he hadn't slept well and had a bit of a headache. He was going to take it easy in preparation for the dance that evening. They talked for a short while, but Joseph seemed a bit uneasy, almost like he was hiding something. She hoped he wasn't withholding bad news or health concerns, but decided fretting over it wouldn't help.

She called Allison to catch up with her and maybe find out if something was worrying Joseph. She got the answering machine after five rings and decided not to leave a message because she really didn't know what to say. Think positive thoughts, she told herself.

All eight residents were present at the dinner table that evening and conversation centered on the Valentine's dance. Everyone was going except for Deborah. She seldom attended evening activities. Actually, she seldom took part in any activities. She was a loner but seemed to be okay with that.

Joseph said that he would come to Sara's apartment at 7:30 to escort her to the party. The residents were looking forward to some nice music from the past, dancing, group games and light refreshments. They peeked into the activity room earlier that afternoon and watched the staff decorate with hearts, balloons and crepe streamers. It looked so festive. Naturally, Jim accepted the DJ job.

Sara returned to her apartment after dinner to get ready. She loved her new red sweater and admired herself in the full-length mirror. She puckered up and blew herself a kiss while her right hand high fived her left. She felt that this was going to be a night to remember.

Joseph gently knocked on her door. She gave him a big hug, not as all-consuming as one of Jan's, but just right, like the porridge, chair and bed that Goldilocks chose. Sara was a bit surprised when Joseph hugged back and planted a kiss on Sara's freshly glossed lips. Wow...this was indeed going to be a night to remember.

The party was just getting started when they arrived. Sara thought she caught a glimpse of Allison at the back of the room but her eyes must have been playing games on her. Family members were not invited to this event. They found two seats at a table close to the DJ area. Jim was reading some announcements. Before he began playing the music he told the partygoers that he had one joke to share.

"Walter walked into a post office just before Valentine's Day. He couldn't help noticing a middle-aged, balding man standing in a corner sticking *Love* stamps on bright pink envelopes with hearts all over them. Then the man got out a bottle of Chanel perfume from his pocket and started spraying scent over the envelopes. By now Walter's curiosity got the better of him so he asked the man why he was sending all those cards. The man replied, 'I'm sending out five-hundred Valentine cards signed, *Guess who?*' 'But why?' asked Walter. The man replied 'I'm a divorce lawyer.'

There were mixed reviews from the residents, but mostly positive this time. Jim bowed to the crowd and then played the first song of the night. It was a slow dance which Sara was very glad to hear. She really enjoyed dancing with Joseph and being held close to him. It made her feel young again and think that anything was possible even though she understood that her remaining life choices were somewhat limited.

She noticed that Joseph was perspiring in spite of the fact that the room was a bit on the cool side. "Joseph, are you feeling all right? You seem to be a little nervous and there's sweat on your forehead, although the room feels rather chilly to me. Maybe we should sit out a couple of dances?"

"I'm fine, Sara. Maybe I shouldn't have worn this blazer or maybe being close to you is causing my engine to overheat!" They returned to their seats after the first two songs played. Jim announced that he was going to turn the microphone over to Joseph for a moment before he dispersed his next round of humor. Joseph approached the makeshift stage and took the microphone in his visibly trembling hands. The room became dead (for lack of a better word) silent and...

Joseph cleared his throat and started to speak but no words came out. He cleared his throat again and put the microphone closer to his mouth. "May I have your attention please? After moving here a year ago I struggled with loneliness, sadness and depression. I thought my life was without purpose. I felt I had no reason to get up each day, no reason to live. Family and friends tried desperately to comfort and console me but to no avail. When I had all but given up, I met someone who brought a ray of sunshine into my dismal, gloomy life. As the months passed, I felt the darkness slowly lift. I questioned it at first but soon accepted the fact that at my ripe old age, I had been hit by Cupid's arrow and was lucky enough to feel genuine love again. Never in my wildest dreams did I ever imagine it would happen.

"So in front of my new friends and family at Parliament Square and my daughter, Allison, I am asking Sara Jennings if she will accept this proposal of marriage. I hope that she will do me the honor of being my bride."

The room was silent as Sara rose from her chair. For a moment she thought that she was having a *what if* moment but no. This was real. She walked up to the stage on legs of Jell-O and took the microphone into her unsteady hands. She looked into Joseph's beautiful blue eyes and said, "What took you so long?"

The guests were on their feet cheering and clapping. There was going to be a wedding at Parliament Square!

Addendum:
Chapter Review
&
Cast of Characters

You Can't Get There From Here is briefly reviewed on the following pages. Each chapter review includes both the real-life event and the corresponding what if moment in Sara's life. Following the review is an alphabetical list of the characters and their roles.

Chapter One: Transition
What If Moment: None

Chapter Two: Reality Check
Real-Life Event: Chose to move to Ireland to live with her father when her parents divorced.

What If Moment: Chose to live with her Mother when her parents divorced and she later died in an airplane accident.

Chapter Three: Acclimation
Real-Life Event: Lost her baby and became unable to conceive more children.

What If Moment: Daughter Kathryn was born healthy and wanted Sara to live with her instead of going to a retirement home when she got too old to live alone.

Chapter Four: Resistance
Real-Life Event: Andrew was killed in the Korean War.

What If Moment: Andrew returned home from the war and he and Sara lived a long, happy, childless life together.

Chapter Five: Dependency
Real-Life Event: Went to nursing school to become a registered nurse after losing Andrew and the baby.

What If Moment: Joined a convent and became a nun.

Chapter Six: Affirmation
Real-Life Event: Had a career as a registered nurse.

What If Moment: Went to medical school and became a pediatrician like her mother.

Chapter Seven: Flirtation
Real-Life Event: Stayed in Massachusetts.

What If Moment: Moved to Florida.

Chapter Eight: Involvement
Real-Life Event: Kevin married his high school sweetheart and broke up with Sara.

What If Moment: Sara married Kevin; they had a wonderful life together and kept each other company into their nineties.

Chapter Nine: Participation
Real-Life Event: Met and married David, her real true love.

What If Moment: David and Sara's paths never crossed.

Chapter Ten: Celebration
What If Moment: None

Chapter Eleven: Anticipation
Real-Life Event: Sara and David decided not to adopt and instead focused on their careers and living life together as a childless couple.

What If Moment: Sara and David adopted a little girl, Cynthia, after her mother died and no relatives could be located. They accepted the challenge and put parenting ahead of their careers.

Chapter Twelve: Acceptance
Real-Life Event: Sara was assigned a college roommate, Michele, who was a woman of color. Although Sara's mother wanted to request a change in roommate, Sara's stepfather insisted that Sara remain with Michele, who became a very good lifelong friend.

What If Moment: Sara was assigned a college roommate, Michele, who was a woman of color and Sara's mother had Sara reassigned to a different room with a white roommate. Sara and Michele did not become friends.

Chapter Thirteen: Reunion
Real-Life Event: The purchase of a house fell through. Instead, Sara and David bought Sara's beloved cottage by the sea.

What If Moment: Sara and David Purchased a house that wasn't located on the ocean and they never got the opportunity to even see the cottage by the sea.

Chapter Fourteen: Disappointment
Real-Life Event: David ran an errand to buy balloons for the mid-winter annual party and was killed by a drunk driver.

What If Moment: Sara discouraged David from running out to buy balloons and they continued to host the mid-winter party for family and friends into their eighties.

Chapter Fifteen: Tradition
Real-Life Event: David had an affair and Sara forgave him his indiscretion. They have a long and happy marriage.

What If Moment: Sara was unable to forgive David for his indiscretion and they divorced.

Chapter Sixteen: Connection
Real-Life Event: Barb, Sara's sister, succumbed to breast cancer at the age of sixty-eight due to late diagnosis.

What If Moment: Barb's breast cancer was caught early and successfully treated.She came to live at the cottage by the sea so Sara wouldn't have to leave her home when she was older.

ELAINE C. BAUMBACH

Chapter Seventeen: Resolution

Real-Life Event: Because they ran late getting to the airport due to Sara's lifelong tardiness, they missed the flight to Egypt and subsequent crash of the airliner.

What If Moment: They were on time for their flight and were killed along with all the other passengers on their flight to Egypt.

Chapter Eighteen: Reflection

Real-Life Event: Joseph did not marry Jean.

What If Moment: Joseph married Jean.

Chapter Nineteen: Conclusion

What If Moment: None

CAST OF CHARACTERS

*(PS indicates Parliament Square
Retirement Village Character)*

Allison
Joseph's daughter, she has two sons.

Andrew
Sara's boyfriend after returning from Ireland. Impregnates Sara out of wedlock, marries her and is then killed in the Korean War on July 14, 1953.

Barbara
Sara's younger sister born in 1942, died in 2010.

Carol
Friend from cottage by the sea, husband still alive.

Celeste (PS)
Resident Bingo addict.

Cindy (PS)
Staff member who is very tall and wears too much makeup.

Cynthia (PS)
Fitness Instructor.

Daniel
Friend and possible love interest during *what if* residency.

David
Sara's second husband born in 1935, died in January 2012.

Deborah (PS)
Tablemate. Perfect, with an accent on affluence.

Diane
Friend from cottage by the sea, husband still alive.

Donald
Pet Airedale Terrier that Sara and David had.

Donna (PS)
Hairdresser.

Emily (PS)
Registered Nurse.

Elizabeth (PS)
Tablemate. Effervescent and friend to all, best friend to Jan, aka Betsy.

Jan (PS)
Tablemate. Outgoing, flashy dresser, best friend to Betsy.

Jean (PS)
Resident. Met on bus to mini golf, interested in Joseph.

Jim (PS)
Tablemate. Talkative, comedian, opinionated.

Joseph (PS)
Tablemate. Crystal blue eyes, handsome, recently widowed. Last name Zimmerman.

Kathryn
Baby Sara lost at birth.

Kevin
Love interest who jilts Sara and marries high school sweetheart.

Kirk
Kathryn's husband in a *what if* moment.

Linda (PS)
Perky social director.

Marcy
Michael's wife.

Mary (PS)
Tablemate. Sun-damaged skin, private, quiet.

Michael
Nephew, Barb's son, Sara's caretaker, born in 1972.

Michele (PS)
College roommate, friend from cottage by the sea.

Pam (PS)
Tablemate. Childlike and friendly.

Penelope
Sara's eight-year-old cat.

Ray
Jean's love interest, last name Adams.

Sara Jennings
Main Character, last name Jennings.

Born: September 10, 1934

Went to Ireland: June 5, 1950 (age 15)

Returned from Ireland: June 1952 (age 17)

Married Andrew: December 1952 (age 18)

Lost baby: June 1953

Lost Andrew: July 1953

Began nursing schoo: 1954

Married David: December 31, 1964 (age 30)

Moved to cottage by the sea: 1976

Moved to Parliament Square: July 2017

Resides in room 316, Parliament Square Retirement Village

Tom
Sara's older brother.

William
Allison's husband

Stay Tuned!

What will the wedding, honeymoon and married life for Sara and Joseph, as newlyweds in their eighties, be like? Will Ray return to Parliament Square and, if he does, will he have a future with Jean? Will Betsy and Jan continue their life-long friendship or will something come between them? Will bingo nights continue or be replaced with something even more exciting? Will Michael and Marcy stay married or will they divorce? Will Cynthia ever get tired? Will Cindy learn how to apply make-up? There are so many questions without answers. Stay tuned. Life at Parliament Square will continue...

Chapter one of the second book in the Parliament Square series, *For Better ... For Worse*, follows. Keep reading to take the next step on the journey with Sara, Joseph and all of their Parliament Square friends.

For Better...For Worse

Chapter One

Cupid Draw Back Your Bow

The initial shock of Joseph's proposal at the Valentine's Day party receded as many of the residents stopped before leaving the party to offer their congratulations and good wishes to Sara and Joseph. In her wildest dreams she couldn't have imagined this happening. Joseph was such a private and reserved gentleman. This was more like one of her what if moments. She had to pinch herself. "Ouch, that hurt." Yes, she really was awake. Joseph proposed to her...she was going to get married. She was going to be Mrs. Sara Jennings Zimmerman.

It was Allison she saw out of the corner of her eye when the evening began. Joseph's daughter was there to witness her father propose to Sara. Allison was overjoyed to see him so happy again. He had mourned the loss of Theresa, his wife and her mother, to the point of self-destruction. At times she feared for his life. Now he was enamored with Sara and eager to author new chapters in their book of life together.

The affection and friendship we feel for others can significantly alter our lives for the better as we age. We don't stop enjoying life when we get old; we get old because we stop enjoying life. Never underestimate the power of the mind.

Our physical strength and abilities may diminish with the aging process, but mind over matter is a powerful motivator. If you think strongly enough that you can do something, it just might be possible.

When Sara and Joseph were alone later that evening, Joseph confessed, "Sara, I didn't want to put you on the spot in front of everyone like I did. My biggest fear was that you would decline my proposal and I thought if I asked you in front of everyone, there was less chance that you'd say no. I realize that I put you in the hot seat and if you said yes just to be polite and not embarrass me in front of everyone, you can still change your mind. I would be so disappointed, but I would understand, or I would at least make every effort to understand. You're a very special lady and although I understand marriage at our age will be challenging and life changing, it's what I want."

"Joseph, you big lummox, of course I accept your proposal. I must admit that I never imagined you getting up in front of everyone and asking me to marry you. You've always been so reserved and quiet. I think everyone else was as surprised as I was. That being said, I'm flattered and honored that you feel two eighty-year-olds have a chance to begin married life together. It's going to be interesting and it might be difficult. There are so many details about us that are uncharted waters to each other. The thought of a man seeing me naked again at my age terrifies me. Even more frightening is the possibility of intimacy. I'm actually afraid to visualize that or ask if it's even possible."

"Sara, we need to take this one step at a time. When you met David and I met Theresa we had the same hurdles to deal with, but they seemed less challenging because we looked younger, we were in good shape, and we couldn't keep our hands off our partners. We're just older versions of those young lovers. What our minds may applaud our bodies might bemoan. It will be a balancing act between what our geriatric minds think we can do and what our seasoned physical bodies will allow us to do. I'm not saying this will be a turnkey operation, but I truly believe in my heart that we are up to making this work. Are you with me, young lady?"

Sara hugged Joseph. "This may sound crazy but I want a wedding here at Parliament Square with all our friends and family. I want it to be a big affair followed by one of those tropical paradise honeymoons at one of those *Sandals* resorts. Of course all the vacationers in the ads are young, tanned and in great shape. We could break the mold there. I think going to a resort like that would be perfect for us. I must admit that I'm afraid to fly, but we'll work on that. Maybe we'd be the oldest newlywed couple ever to reserve their honeymoon suite.

"They have a bar in the pool that you can swim up to and order a glass of wine while in your bathing suit. I could even wear a two-piece bathing suit…no, no, no… just kidding. I don't want to distract those younger boys from their new wives. We'll make lots of memories, the majority of which—*ahem*—we'll share with our family and friends. If we're going to do this, we're going to do it right. Being past your prime doesn't mean we can't enjoy life. It just means we may have to experience it a little more slowly. But you know what? Some things are worth slowing down for."

The time passed quickly as they discussed plans for their wedding and honeymoon. It was exciting. It would be the talk of the town. It provided something to look forward to in this over-the-hill, often mundane community. It was going to be an event the residents of Parliament Square would remember for a long, long time. It definitely wasn't something that happened frequently. Funerals, 911 calls and hospital visits, yes. Weddings, bridal showers and honeymoons, no.

Joseph escorted Sara to her room. He embraced her tightly and gently pressed his lips to hers. This was the beginning of a new chapter in both of their lives.

No one knows how their final chapter in life will end with the exception of those who choose to self-destruct. Some hope for good health and longevity, others feel money is the answer, but companionship in later years is the real secret to happiness. There is truth in the saying, "money can't buy happiness." Having a significant other next to you at night, to share meals and conversation with, and to be there for you in the morning when you awaken, provides a true sense of security and an inner peace. Being married later in life is underrated. It can make all the difference in the world.

Sara chatted with Penelope. "We are going to expand our family. You'll like Joseph. I'm not sure if he's a cat person, but we'll convert him if he isn't. You're like family to me and your companionship has helped me during this difficult transition period. Now Joseph is going to join us and make life even better. I'm once again going to be someone's wife. I never thought I'd have feelings again for another man. I thought David was my one and only after I lost Andrew. It turns out I was wrong."

It was late and Sara was very tired. She nestled into bed with Penelope by her side. She expected a moment from the past to surface but nothing materialized. She fell into a deep sleep as she cuddled her pillow. Soon she would have someone to hold her at night once again. This wasn't a dream. This was really happening.

The morning sun illuminated the room. Cold winter wind bent the tree branches outside the window and cast dancing shadows on the wall. Inside her heart it was warm. It wasn't the kind of warmth controlled by the thermostat. It was the kind of warmth that comes from a fire burning deep within the soul. It was going to be a wonderful day. The birds sang outside the window and Penelope was curled in a ball on the pillow beside her, purring loudly.

Sara was a bit overwhelmed thinking about all that had to be done before the wedding. She didn't want to go to the courthouse for a civil ceremony. She wanted to marry Joseph in the Parliament Square chapel with their friends and family present. She wanted to walk down the aisle as the wedding march played. She wanted Michael to be her escort. Michael! She hadn't told him! He just had to attend the wedding. She would plan it around his schedule if she had to. She couldn't get married without him. He was her closest relative. She'd call him a bit later since he was on the West Coast and it was still quite early there.

They needed to select invitations and plan a reception. She needed to decide who would be in her wedding party, definitely Michele and possibly Allison. She remembered the gowns Jan and Betsy wore in her *what if* moment when Jean married Joseph. She shook that from her mind. No one wearing those gaudy bridesmaid dresses and headpieces would be part of her wedding party. Maybe just two attendants would be enough. She didn't want to go overboard. She and Joseph needed to select a date. First she had to talk with Michael to find out what date would work for him. Yes, she would start there. Her head spun as the realization of the wedding gelled in her brain. This was really going to happen, and sooner than later. They weren't getting any younger.

After a quick shower Sara went to the dining room for breakfast. She was starving. As she walked to her table Linda literally jogged toward her calling her name. "Sara, Sara, I have great news." Sara turned and Linda almost ran her over as she attempted to stop. "I was chatting with a friend of mine at the local news channel this morning and mentioned the good news about Joseph proposing to you last evening. My friend talked to her superior at the station and they want to interview you two for the evening news. She said they might ask to attend the wedding and put it on TV. Isn't that great news? Isn't that exciting? You, Joseph and all the folks here at Parliament Square on television. How great would that be?" This was a lot to process before her first cup of coffee. Sara didn't want to appear ungrateful. "Thanks, but I have to talk to Joseph about this. We're a couple now and we make our decisions together." As the words came out of her mouth the reality of the situation slapped her in the face. She was no longer able to answer without consulting her 'other half.' She was again going to be part of a couple. She liked that. She missed David, but she didn't realize until this very moment that she missed even more being someone's wife. That was all about to change.

The dining room was abuzz with conversation about the proposal and the upcoming wedding. All eyes were on Sara as she took her seat. Joseph was already there and he glanced at her with his beautiful blue eyes. My what a difference a day makes. The players were the same but the stakes had changed drastically. Their table would have a married couple seated there in the months to come. She would no longer be Sara Jennings. She would be Sara Jennings Zimmerman.

Jan insisted on giving Sara one of her over-the-top hugs to congratulate her on her upcoming nuptials, which looked nice but caused Sara to gasp for air and fight to regain normal breathing. Jan certainly was a strong hugger. Joseph seemed relieved when she returned to her seat and didn't head over in his direction.

Sara thought that there were three categories of huggers. The limp noodle hugger allows someone to hug them but basically provides little or no return of affection. If given a choice, they would definitely rather shake hands or high-five instead of hugging. The second category was the middle-of-the-road hugger. They respond based on the level of hug received. If hugged lightly, they return a light hug. If hugged firmly, they return a firm hug. They also don't initiate the hug in most cases. The final and third category is the all-consuming hug-like-your-life-depends- upon-it hugger. They engage quickly without warning and squeeze with unwarranted strength and control. Their embrace lasts too long and the recipient struggles to get free and regain rhythmic breathing. Jan was definitely a member of category three.

The conversation quickly turned to the proposal and upcoming wedding. Deborah was brought up to speed since she hadn't attended the Valentine's Day event. Pam asked Joseph, "Did you give Sara an engagement ring? I didn't see any ring last evening." Sara never even thought about that. A ring would be nice. She still wore her engagement and wedding rings as she felt in her heart she was still married to David. That would have to change now. She needed to remove them permanently and she felt that David would understand. She had a new man in her life now.

Spouses are like pets. You may choose another after losing one but that new one never replaces the old one. Each is special in its own way. Your life goes on with the new spouse or new pet, but in your heart there will always be a special place for the departed one. It wasn't disrespectful to the departed spouse but rather a part of the healing process for the survivor. For some it happens quickly, for some it takes time and for others it never happens.

Joseph replied to Pam, "I want Sara to select her engagement ring. I'm not good at such things and my daughter advised me to have Sara go with me to the jewelry store. Allison will take us shopping next week. I want Sara to select the nicest ring in the store. I want to be able to see it shine on her finger from across the room. She deserves nothing but the best."

Sara remembered Allison telling her about the wealth Joseph and Theresa had accumulated. Sara was concerned because parental wealth can become a hot button when a parent remarries later in life. If something happened to Joseph (hopefully many years from now), Sara didn't want to inherit money that should be passed on to his daughter and her family. She would discuss this with Joseph and ask that he have a prenuptial agreement drawn up stating that the majority of his wealth at the time of his demise would go to Allison. That was the right thing to do. She was certainly not a gold digger and didn't want what wasn't rightfully hers. There were so many items to be added to the list and checked off prior to saying their wedding vows.

After breakfast Sara excused herself and returned to her apartment. She was so anxious to call Michael and tell him the wonderful news. She definitely wanted him to escort her down the aisle. He and Joseph would look so handsome in their wedding tuxedoes.

Michael answered the telephone on the third ring. He asked if anything was wrong because calling him early in the morning was out of character. She said, "Everything's fine. In fact everything's much better than fine. Everything is wonderful. Joseph asked me to marry him last evening at the Valentine's Day dance and I accepted. Your old Aunt Sara is getting married!" There was a long silence at the other end of the phone. Didn't Michael hear what she said? Was there a bad connection?

"Aunt Sara, I am so happy for you. I'm just a bit surprised. I didn't know you and Joseph were at this point in your relationship. Are you sure marriage is what you really want right now? You just got comfortable with living at Parliament Square. This will be another major adjustment. Marriage isn't always a bed or roses. At your age or at any age it's a challenge. I don't want to be a wet blanket and rain on your parade but

I also don't want to see you unhappy because you decided in haste to accept his proposal."

"Michael, I appreciate your honesty and concern, but at my age I don't have time to try to figure out if I'm doing the right thing. Whether Joseph and I have days, months or years together as a married couple, I want it to start as soon as possible. We don't have the option of exploring our relationship during a long engagement. That's for younger couples. We need to enjoy each other's company starting yesterday and pray that we have many tomorrows together. Nothing in life is guaranteed. I lost Andrew less than a year after we married. Whatever time Joseph and I have together will be the butter-cream icing on my cake of life."

"You sound pretty certain. You convinced me. I am really happy for you. What date have you set for the big event? I want to be there to see you as the beautiful bride. Maybe I could even have the honor of escorting you down the aisle. What do you think?"

"Michael, I called to ask if you would do me the honor or walking me down the aisle. I can't imagine getting married without you here. Check your datebook and we'll set a date when you can fly back here for the wedding. What does your April schedule look like?"

"Let me check my calendar and call you back. I think Saturday, April 14th looks good, but I want to make sure. Also, on a different subject, Marcy decided the West Coast wasn't for her. She left last week. I'm not sure when or if she'll return. We have our issues and maybe this is for the best. I'm giving the situation some time before making any permanent decisions. I always felt that you and Mother didn't approve of Marcy. She's not perfect, but then again neither am I."

"I am so sorry to hear that, Michael. I'll pray for you both. Check your availability for April and call me by the end of the week please. Your old aunt is going to be a bride again. I had to pinch myself to believe it was really happening."

When their conversation ended Sara felt both happy and sad. Michael would be returning for the wedding, but his marriage hit a rough patch. Although she didn't think Marcy was a good match for him, it's hard when any marriage ends. Hopefully there would be a happy ending for him with or without Marcy. He deserved to be happy.

Once there was confirmation from Michael about April 14th, the wheels would start turning to reserve the chapel, a location for the reception, order the wedding invitations, decide on the bridal party...and the list went on and on. There would certainly be nothing boring or empty about life at Parliament Square for Sara or Joseph in the coming months. Life would be very busy. That was good.

molly's place rescue

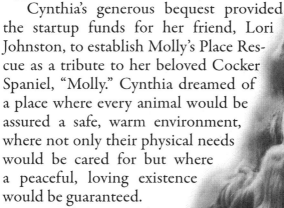

Cynthia Lane Magaro and I became friends at a young age when I moved to Pennsylvania in the fourth grade. Our friendship grew as we attended Highland Elementary, Lemoyne Middle School and Cedar Cliff High School together. I sat next to Cynthia at the last class reunion she attended. Unfortunately, she was taken from us much too soon.

Cynthia was a devoted animal welfare advocate whose untimely departure from this Earth as a result of a battle with cancer was a tragedy to both her two and four-legged friends, and she is dearly missed.

Cynthia's generous bequest provided the startup funds for her friend, Lori Johnston, to establish Molly's Place Rescue as a tribute to her beloved Cocker Spaniel, "Molly." Cynthia dreamed of a place where every animal would be assured a safe, warm environment, where not only their physical needs would be cared for but where a peaceful, loving existence would be guaranteed.

Over the years I have contributed food and

other items to this no-kill rescue and I will donate a portion of the profits from book sales as well.

Please consider making your own contribution to Molly's Place Rescue.

Learn more at
www.MollysPlaceRescue.org.

Molly's Place Rescue
5220 East Trindle Road
Mechanicsburg, PA 17050

(717) 691-5555

MollysPlace@Verizon.net

<u>Hours</u>
Wednesday 12:00 – 4:00
Friday 12:00 – 4:00
Saturday 12:00 – 4:00
Sunday 12:00 – 4:00

Closed Monday, Tuesday,
and Thursday

molly's place rescue

About the Author

ELAINE C. BAUMBACH was born in Whitestone, New York; transplanted to Camp Hill, Pennsylvania in the fourth grade; and has lived in Central Pennsylvania ever since. After college, she embarked on a career in information technology which spanned forty-plus years. During that time, Elaine dabbled in writing, nurturing a gift she discovered during her early journalism classes in high school.

The responsibilities of family, work, and life consumed her schedule for decades and writing was put on the backburner until recently, when authoring a novel bubbled to the top of her bucket list. Elaine lives with her husband, James, and their furry family member, Andrew, in New Cumberland, Pennsylvania. A portion of all proceeds from *You Can't Get There From Here* will benefit Molly's Place Rescue of Mechanicsburg, Pennsylvania.

29404631R00137

Made in the USA
Middletown, DE
22 December 2018